MW01047563

Tales of Wonder

Gracie and the Wacky Bunch

A Comedy, a Mystery
and a Love Story

First and Possibly Surely Maybe
Final Draft

Ordinary Fabulous
Literary Work of Art... (yep)

by

Richard R. Wyly, Sr.

Tales of Wonder: Gracie and the Wacky Bunch
Copyright © 2020 by Richard R. Wyly, Sr.

Tellwell Talent
www.tellwell.ca

ISBN
978-0-2288-3171-6 (Hardcover)
978-0-2288-3169-3 (Paperback)
978-0-2288-3170-9 (eBook)

Reviews

Tales of Wonder: Gracie and the Wacky Bunch

"A must-read for everyone who lived and loved the Woodstock era! Richard Wyly's creative and colorful stream of consciousness is a worthy trip (pun intended!). A uniquely captivating literary romp."

— Darcey-Lynn MacArthur
Entrepreneur and Chief Cookie Maker

"This book is truly bizarre... beautifully bizarre! A vividly told story of a magical journey with a wild and wacky bunch! It's cagily creative. The author transformed a bird named Augie and a cat named Spike into almost humanlike beings that we came to love and adore. The opening description of Haight-Ashbury and San Francisco carried through to the portrayals of the characters and the scenes they found themselves in, creating an ongoing movie of the mind. Mr. Wyly covertly delivered on some deeply personal and romantic relationships, as witnessed by the connections between Lucinda, Graham, KK Bailey and Gracie."

— Bob MacArthur
Retired Healthcare CEO

"Richard Wyly has a unique and colorful sense of humor, leading the reader into a zany world of crazy characters and places. He makes you feel as if you're experiencing part of a movie screenplay. Mel Brooks would be proud."

— Mike Gould
Professional photographer

"His writing reminiscent of Tom Robbins, Richard Wyly creates a world filled with wild and colourful characters who are sent on a mission impossible. Hilarious and unexpected turns keep the reader on a roller-coaster ride. A funny and entertaining read. It will leave you with a smile on your face."

— Wayne Grams
Information Services Coordinator, ret.,
Alberta Parks, Canada

"Oh my, these *Tales of Wonder* and folk tale Sagas by Richard Wyly go a lick beyond humor — for the precise reason that their purpose is to 'mess with your mind.' The list of characters in his second book, *Gracie and the Wacky Bunch*, for one thing, boggles the mental imagery potential of the human brain; second up are the names of these folks; and third... the CIA, Interpol and MI6 investigation into all the people around the globe who've succumbed to the 'Vapor Domes of Death.' Such is the theme of the book, couched in humor and evil, which will keep the reader tantalized and humorized by the comedy, the mystery and the love story which are the heartbeat and soul of this adventure. So many characters getting into myriad deeds of mischief written as only Richard Wyly can write. Enjoy."

— Terry M. Wilmot, Ph.D.

Praise for Richard Wyly's First Book,
Tales of Wonder: The Saga of Stickitville

(Rated 4 stars out of a possible 5 by IndieReader)

"Does the story make sense? Not always. Is it entertaining? Absolutely.... In addition to his keen sense of humor, author Richard Wyly is skilled at providing just the right descriptive touches to bring his characters (and their town) to life."

— Lisa Butts for IndieReader

"This book is a good read for a weekend afternoon plagued with poor weather. All the quirky characters one could encounter in a lifetime enter the pages without need for long explanations — they just 'are'. The story romps hilariously from antic to antic, festival to festival, revealing the citizens of Stickitville and their intertwined lives and dubious habits (yucca dust) without dragging the reader into poetically descriptive narratives. You — the reader — become a participant, stuffing any gaps with recollections of personal encounters with such characters in years past. *Tales of Wonder: The Saga of Stickitville* could become a new cult classic."

— Colleen Campbell
Artist

In loving memory of my brother,

Victor L. Wyly, Jr.

1936–2018

Table of Contents

Introduction

The initial setting for this outrageous adventure is the San Francisco Bay Area — more specifically, a community known as the Haight-Ashbury district. Sometimes the story jumps across the Golden Gate Bridge to the charming enclaves of the Sausalito Marina and Tiburon.

"The Haight" was a well-known haven in the 1960s for the drug-crippled and the downtrodden, as well as for some very creative poets and novelists — including Allen Ginsberg and Jack Kerouac, recognized by many as the father of the Beat Generation — and for musicians, artists and defiant future politicians. The neighborhood spawned such notable greats as Janis Joplin, Carlos Santana, Neil Young, John Denver, Arlo Guthrie, Joe Cocker, Richie Havens, Joan Baez, Bob Dylan, Jimi Hendrix and Ravi Shankar. Among the amazing bands that were part of this movement were Crosby, Stills and Nash; Creedence Clearwater Revival; the Grateful Dead; the Who; Grace Slick and the Jefferson Airplane; Chicago; Blood, Sweat and Tears; the Allman Brothers Band; and many others. Several of these iconic music legends performed at the Fillmore West, a historical venue in San Francisco.

All of this had to happen, or — guess what — no Woodstock. Not sure why we had to go clear across the country for the concert to happen, but we did anyway. Many got lost; surprisingly, millions didn't. Actually, the attendance number hangs somewhere around a half a million. We will never know, because dumb-ass Marvin Schlinker's hand-operated tally clicker broke due to too much clicking; he never lubed anything on time. He said it was under warranty but it wouldn't be fixed soon enough. Marvin was grateful for the break, as both of his thumbs were badly blistered.

Right about now, you probably know I'm gonna be messing with your head, don't ya? (Maynard's already rolling his eyes.)

There were a couple of hotshot speech-making dudes who heavily influenced the youth culture in the Bay Area, as well as much of the rest of our country. Eventually, a lot of the world also got the message of impending social change — at least in the places that had radios, TVs, record players and godawful eight-track tape players.

Two of these modern gurus were Timothy Leary and my favorite, Richard Alpert, later known as "Ram Dass." Dr. Tim taught us about something called LSD and how to "turn on, tune in and drop out." Ram Dass wrote a book titled *Be Here Now*. I still read it from time to time, and I can seriously recommend that you consider doing the same.

Whoa! "Stop the presses," as the saying goes. I must not go any further with this rambling review of historical events tied to the Haight and other places in California, without mentioning a very important person. There was this giant figure of an enlightened man who stunned his faithful followers by sharing his own "Tales of Wonder" experiences. He was none other than Dr. Carlos Castaneda, a professor at UCLA who lectured in the anthropology department. His classes were packed with wide-eyed students eager to listen and learn. Carlos introduced us to a man known as don Juan Matus, a Yaqui Indian who lived in the Sonoran Desert in Mexico. He was considered to be a "man of knowledge." Castaneda wrote about his experiences with him, including living in a separate reality by ingesting mescalito and peyote, psychotropic plants that will most definitely alter normal consciousness. If you read nothing else, then at least read his first three books — simply fascinating. Those of you who already "know" don't have to thank me, but I appreciate it; you might want to read them again, refresh, dream. I believe that don Juan could still be out there, in one form or another.

* * *

The main characters in this glorified romp of an adventure are as follows:

1. Gracie Aylene McNichols, our special heroine and a fighter against evil
2. Kouba Kenta Bailey, our resident albino, an explosives expert and a mentor to Gracie
3. Lucinda May Obermeyer, Gracie's mom and the life-mate of Graham McNichols
4. Graham Reginald McNichols, ex-hippie, now US Senator and Gracie's dad
5. Augie McFarland, Graham's paranoid parakeet

6. Spike O'Malley, Graham's seventy-pound calico pussycat, and Augie's nemesis (*Seventy pounds! ...Really?*)
7. Quinella Louise Fitzpatrick, a mysterious creation from Lucinda's genome
8. O'Gooha Bhah Tootoe, an 8-foot, 7-inch Zulu prince and CIA operative known as "Chubby"
9. Beto and Chaco Bailarín, identical twins and the evil leaders of "The Shadow Dancers"
10. Clara O'Donald, ex-navy fighter pilot caught up in the Dancers' web
11. Farley Arkle, trapped pot-smoking limo driver, often lost
12. Merle, part-time caretaker at the Soup and Burger Emporium
13. Dexter Offenduzzum, traitor and snitch, occasional private jet host
14. "Packy the Pickle," devious five-star server at the Pine Inn in Carmel
15. Dottie Monet, bank robber and famous TV cult hero
16. Nelda Zaffley, world-renowned concert pianist
17. Ralph, clothing nut obsessed with a guy on horseback swinging a club

18. Dino and Luigi, owners of the trendy Chef Boy-O'-Boy Steakhouse and Pub
19. Dr. Hal Hankerbee, phoney shrink assigned to evaluate Lucinda's personality disorder
20. Judge Aaron K. Ledbetter, Graham's corrupt, goofy golfing buddy
21. Melinda Slipindonker, a dumped and very angry volleyball captain
22. Garth McTavish, a skeleton on a motorcycle in Chubby's fish aquarium
23. The Entity, a.k.a. "He, who is Him," a cosmic blue-fiber being
24. Maynard, a mysterious visionary and itinerant man of knowledge

Prologue

Gracie Aylene McNichols was the 14-year-old daughter of Senator Graham Reginald McNichols and his wife, Lucinda, right here in Rushtuk, Idaho. Gracie's mom was known as Lucinda May, and she was about to be released from the mental ward that housed the criminally insane at the Rushtuk Women's Penitentiary. Lucinda was the only surviving member of the wealthy Benjamin Franklin Obermeyer family. They were billionaires and controlled two fifths of the world's oil supply. The family also owned all of the raw forest lands in the Pacific Northwest.

Lucinda's condition, and the reason for her being incarcerated, was uncommon and complex: multiple psychotic personalities; involvement with drugs; bank robberies; and performing as a concert pianist named Nelda Zaffely. Lucinda also posed as the media-created rock star bank robber known as Dottie Monet. In addition, she sold fake IDs to a loose band of so-called American Patriots. They were in fact drug abusers and dealers. Patriots, not so much. They were really bad people — "crooked crooks," if you will — and the worst of their kind; even their animals were bad. That was easy to understand, as their "pets" were mostly pit bull–mix dogs that never got enough to eat. Their cats were even meaner: they were forced to catch their own mice and small birds and snakes. Occasionally, the cats would sneak food from the pit bulls, putting their lives in mortal danger. Pit bulls are not above eating cats for lunch or simply having them as a tasty snack.

Rushtuk is a township of about 25,000 residents. It's situated in a lovely valley with snow-covered mountaintops, trout streams, lakes and duck ponds. The local farmers mostly grow Golden apples for export, along with Peaches and Cream corn, assorted veggies and a lot of "weed," and we sincerely mean *a lot of weed*. It's Rushtuk's most profitable crop by far but not quite legal just yet.

Peaceful and normal on the surface, Rushtuk appeared to be a great place to raise a family. The truth of the matter was that beneath this charming image lurked all kinds of evil stuff.

Gracie was young, amazingly bright and very aware for a 14-year-old. She had a sense of what was going on and would wear a friendly but knowledgeable "face smirk" about the community's deception. Folks would try and pretend to cover up certain truths. She was way ahead of all of them.

Gracie Aylene's father was Idaho's State Senator, Graham Reginald McNichols, now 45 years old. He wore dark blue pinstripe suits, and his dress shirts were lightly starched, all-cotton Oxford cloth. He liked wingtip-style leather shoes in a cordovan color. His neckties were handmade by Talbot of Carmel, California.

This was the Senator's "working warrior" attire when he was doing the public's business right there in the Idaho Senate building. On Fridays, he would drag out his navy cashmere blazer by Norman Hilton with a colorful silk pocket square. Holding up his gray slacks were braided leather suspenders by Trafalgar, or possibly a Coach leather belt. He would choose a tattersall open-collar shirt from Robert Stock. A very casual look, finished off with Bass Weejun penny loafers and no socks. He said it was a fashion tip he had learned from Elliot Gant — or was it Bert Pulitzer?

In checking out our resident politician's credentials, we find that in his late teen years and early twenties he lived right smack in the middle of the Haight-Ashbury district, not too far from downtown San Francisco. Good ol' Graham looked a bit different back in those days. Certainly different from the way our polished-up, straight-arrow "politico" guy looked now. Did I mention that he also wore tortoiseshell-frame glasses that were made with clear lenses and a 20-20 prescription? It was all for show, which of course meant that he didn't need glasses at all. It was obviously a traditional prop used solely to enhance his personal appearance.

This was one cool fashion-plate dude. He probably talked to "Ralph" a lot. Ya think? Thus, lessons were learned from the "great book" of "Designer Schtick 101," including a gentleman's guide to the natural-shoulder lifestyle. (Maynard prefers Levi's model 501 prewashed-denim basic jeans, to be worn pulled down over his Rios handmade alligator skin cowboy boots.)

Well, back in his youth, Graham had long, wavy brownish hair that came down about four inches past his shoulders and was still growing. His beard was fashionably full and Biblical in appearance. He could have easily been mistaken for a disciple from Nazareth. In his dreams he was sure he had been one of them. It would have been a very long time ago, in another life, at the Last Supper, which by the way was the annual social event held at the "Mount of Olives Bistro," a place that was famous for sermons. Graham imagined that in the giant mural behind the large dinner table — which, incidentally, was signed by Mickey Angelo — he was the fourth Apostle from the left of JC.

A moderate-size gold earring was punched through the lobe of his left ear to complement the "head look," as it was called back in the '60s. He always wore bold-floral-print all-polyester long-sleeved shirts tucked into his faded blue denim bell-bottom jeans. He had a collection of several gold chains around his neck, with a dolphin pendant attached to one of them. Lots of wrist bracelets, and rings on his fingers. Shoes were either the side-buckle stacked platforms with really high heels, or his trusty light blue worn-out Nike runners. His winter jacket was a dark brown brushed suede leather. It was the Western-cut model with lots of fringe stringers jingling and jangling about as he wandered in and around San Francisco's Bay Area. Some people claimed it was the very jacket that had been stolen from *The Mayan*, David Crosby's famous schooner, where some say the classic album *Wooden Ships* was composed. The boat was usually moored over in Sausalito. ...Hmmm!

Graham worked as a special-events writer and a delivery boy for the *Los Angeles Free Press*. This weekly counterculture publication specialized in reporting on the "hippie" lifestyle and was laced with silly but poignant random writings relentlessly attacking the arrogant and stuffy all-controlling establishment.

The *Free Press* newspaper had a huge and amazingly dedicated following. Its left-leaning social content ran up and down the West Coast and reached the pot-smoking rock crowd's impressionable youth. The job didn't pay a whole lot, but Graham could get high all day and still do the work more or less on time. He made plenty of money selling weed and other mind-expanding, brain-whacking goodies. He never sold anything that he hadn't tried out on himself first, just to check out its powers and promise. He said it was part of the customer service and a loyalty commitment to his personal market.

Graham's philosophy was to not do any drugs other than pot during the week. He felt weekends should be reserved for heavy mind-altering experiences, like attending rock concerts, doing some acid or perhaps munching down a handful of mushrooms. A special treat, and really easy to do, would be to toast up a couple of chunky peanut butter and grape jelly sandwiches. Back in those days, they were plentiful.

Graham liked and respected both LSD and mescaline when "dropped" into his system. In the early-morning hours he could choose either, as there were many types to select from. His acid favorites were "Orange Barrel," "Purple Microdot," "Silver Lady" and "Windowpane." There were many other varieties out there, but you had to be careful and know your source, or *you* just might not be *you* anymore.

Mescaline can have a sobering effect after about eight hours of power zooming. To add variety to this sensational experience, you could enhance some of the very intense and brightly colored visual vibrations by simply reloading your system with a fistful of psilocybin magic mushrooms. It would pick up the moment and send you right back out there for another eight hours or so. At this point no one was counting. Sometimes it could be difficult to climb back down from the intense, shimmering rainbows that were clattering around inside your head.

One not so memorable weekend, Graham decided to see what might happen if he took all four of his special brain-socket actuators at the same time. He had planned to go to the historic Monterey Pop Festival, about an hour south of San Francisco. Well, due to the "cocktail" kicking in early, he never made it down the steps of his apartment to hop onto his Vespa scooter then ride over to the Greyhound bus depot.

The hours seemed to blow by in an instant. Later, when Graham could actually put a sentence together again, he realized that this "fuzzy-wuzzy-buzzy" day was history and long gone. Well, he said he had a good time, anyway, discussing all manner of interesting things such as politics, women, food, cars and landscaping with his paranoid parakeet, named Augie McFarland. Graham claimed he always learned a lot from him. As a treat he would always give the bird the leftover stems and seeds from his depleted pot stash. The parakeet seemed thankful and would crackle his beak in a back-and-forth sawing motion, making terrible messes on the floor of his cage.

Augie was always sort of moody and fidgety. He often had to deal with mild depression. He seemed to sigh a lot, then he would always follow this expression with a slow eye blink. Some days he would sit for hours on one or more of the perch swings in his cage. Occasionally, the parakeet could be seen lifting a leg and leaning to one side. Then in a flash he would let a well-timed butt-ripper load up and blast into the room, delivering one of his best feather-ruffling bird farts. Graham would sit for hours — laughing, waiting, rolling joints and hoping to catch it all on video.

There was another perfectly good reason Augie was always so freaked out. Graham almost never remembered to close the door of the bird cage when leaving the apartment. Augie liked the fact that he could fly around at will when Graham was home; that was fun, and feeling the freedom was great. Here was the problem: Graham also had a huge calico tomcat named Spike O'Malley. This feline sucker weighed in right at 70 pounds — huge for your garden-variety calico pussycat, for sure.

Spike would torment Augie whenever he felt like being self-entertained. He was obviously too obese to leap up and snatch the tasty little bird. Our tomcat would saunter back and forth in front of the elevated cage, occasionally looking up, making eye contact, licking his lips and showing his razor-sharp teeth. There was the winking and endless communicating that went something like this: "Someday little dude, it's gonna happen — you know it, I know it, we both know it." *Yummy-yummy-pucky, parakeet-tasty-crunchy little Augie bird dipped in paw-paw sauce.* Spike described it as "larapin.'" (Even Maynard had to go look this one up.)

Hmmm! Our spunky ol' calico tomcat would imagine this scenario almost daily.

Once Graham was on his way to feeling straight again, he wandered back to the bathroom. When he flushed the toilet it scared the dickens out of him. He swore that multiple three-foot-long yellow and red flames spiraled upward, hissed and leapt out of the bowl right at him. Augie, also high, screeched uncontrollably because the whole room seemed to be pulsing in flashing colors. Yep, a little "Purple Microdot" will definitely enhance your visual experiences all day long. Graham knew something wasn't right, so he drank several beers and chased them down with José Cuervo Gold shooters. Finally, everything was okay... (Uh-huh. "You betchum, Red Ryder," said Little Beaver.)

A few years earlier, Graham had attended a lecture at Berkley to hear Dr. Timothy Leary rattle on about psychedelic drugs and their future in psychiatric medicine. Mostly, Graham learned that you could survive and function more or less normally on just four brain cells. Should you slide down to only three, you became cerebral mush and would have to look at your driver's licence to see who the heck you were. That's, of course, if you still had a driver's licence. Perhaps you could find a friend to vouch for you — assuming they could do the same for themselves.

Chapter One

Rushtuk Hi-jinks and Romance

Our future Senator finally packed in the Bay Area hippy-dippy lifestyle. He cut off the long hair and shaved the beard. He drove over to the Goodwill Thrift Store and dropped off his collection of denim bell-bottom jeans, the flowered shirts, the platform side-buckle shoes with the super-high heels, and the worn-out Nike runners. He pawned the chains and rings and wrist bracelets. He kept the gold chain with the dolphin pendant as a keepsake.

In an emotional moment, Graham drove over to the Golden Gate Bridge, parked the car and walked across about halfway. Slowly, he teased off the earring with the engraved initials GRM from its "home on the lobe." The shiny ring had graced his left ear, which clearly represented the "hippie culture" and the "head look" for many years and was what made him a part of that lifestyle. He placed the earring down flat on the guardrail of the bridge, facing the Alcatraz Federal Penitentiary. With a silver dollar held in both hands, he pinched down on the edge of the earring with his thumbs and Tiddlywinked it into the San Francisco Bay.

We're not sure, but there was this weird fish story that later surfaced in the *Free Press*. Apparently, a lost chub mackerel from Mexico on its way to Alaska to spawn was hit on the snout by a mini-missile gold earring and the stupid fish swallowed it. Seventeen days later, some Native kids fishing off the cliffs near Juneau, Alaska, caught the mackerel, promptly barbecued it and sold the earring with the engraved initials GRM for 23 dollars. It was a good day for the local Tlingit kids. (Maynard says it's pronounced "Klink-gett" or "Klink-ett.")

* * *

Leaving his friends behind in San Francisco and especially Haight-Ashbury would prove to be more difficult for Graham than he had imagined. There were so many memories, even the ones that were not remembered due to sometimes massive drug interference but that were still being given respectable space. Graham returned to his apartment with a freshly shaved face, sans long hair and earring. Augie the parakeet freaked out 'cause he didn't know who in the heck this dude was. Likewise, Spike the obese cat tried to hide under the couch but was too fat and got himself stuck in the process. Both Augie and Graham laughed themselves silly. The yuk-yuks helped Graham get over leaving for the next big adventure. It was truly time for a change. Here we come, Rushtuk, Idaho — you ain't seen nothing yet.

Graham had stayed in touch with one of his old Army buddies who was already living in Rushtuk doing odd jobs for the police department and the bowling alley. His name was Kouba Kenta Bailey. He was an albino immigrant from Nigeria. We're not certain how this Kouba Kenta guy got into the US Army, seeing as how he still had a six-inch chicken leg bone poked horizontally through his upper lip just under his nose. He had intense pink eyes and a stacked-up, curly all-white Rastafarian-style hairdo featuring the latest trend of long "Bob Marley" dreadlocks.

The Army recruiting station in San Francisco had seen a lot of things over the years, but we're pretty sure this one got both the blue ribbon and the gold trophy. With all the draft-dodging taking place, they were accepting just about anybody in the late '60s and early '70s. Kouba Kenta Bailey ended up being a First Sergeant in charge of high-level explosives. This would become helpful and very interesting in the coming years. (Sorry, you will have to wait to see exactly why. It's worth it — be patient, have a toke.)

They became great pals again. On one visit, before the move to Idaho, Kouba Kenta even learned how to ride Graham's Vespa. Crashing it was part of learning, and the old scooter had seen better days anyhow, so it didn't really matter. Graham just worried about him getting hurt. One afternoon, Kouba was blasting down one of San Francisco's famous steep hills and T-boned a local taxicab. The crash pole-vaulted him over the top of the cab and right into the middle of a trolley car going in the opposite direction. He ended up with his face being smacked, smothered and crammed right down to where it began bouncing up and back, then back and forth. He was jammed in nose first, and nearly suffocated. Our shocked Mr. Bailey found himself wadded up neatly between two screaming transvestites who were completely freaked out.

Kouba Kenta Bailey

In keeping with San Francisco cablecar tradition, you could be a long-haired zoomie and probably still work while being quite stoned. You could be a shaggy, hippy-dippy cablecar conductor who might nonchalantly ask for a full fare from Kouba Kenta, the big-bone Bailey. Never mind the crash or Graham's beloved crunched-up Vespa. Well, if Kouba couldn't pay with tokens, he would have to get off at the next stop.

The sassy "lipstick lassies" were blown away by all of this; we're sure it was the chicken bone (he still wore it when off duty) or the fact that he was an albino. They invited him to dinner before the next stop. (This is good stuff, Maynard.)

* * *

Kouba Kenta Bailey helped Graham move over to Rushtuk, where they set up his new apartment. They made Augie and Spike feel as much at home as was possible. Augie was nervous, and Spike was checking out all the angles for launching an attack on the paranoid parakeet. He kept throwing kisses at Augie and nodding his huge head up and down as if to say, "It's going to be soon, my little feathered friend." Augie just glared and gave him the traditional feather finger as best he could and called him a big, fat, stupid punk and an ugly pussycat. (Parakeets can talk, ya know.)

This is as good a time as any to give you, my astute and cherished readers, some additional information on Graham's pets. It's not a small thing, so pay attention. Spike, the 70-pound calico pussycat, simply showed up at McNichols' one Sunday morning dragging a world-class trophy mouse. He dropped it on the porch and then laid out a string of morbid and sorrowful but melodic meows, possibly inspired by old Gaelic folksongs. Moved to tears, a psychologically sucker-punched Graham took the grumpy ol' snaggle-puss in as a trusted pet.

Augie the paranoid parakeet was purchased at the annual Haight-Ashbury snake and bird swap meet. Graham paid some weirdo dude four bucks and half a lid of Mexican weed for this shy handful of feathers. What he didn't know was that Augie had been infected with a rare bird disease called *Gigantus Soonus Non Fitus in da Cageous*. (Maynard said that he had seen this before and that some of the afflicted parakeets could grow to the size of a chicken hawk.) As you will see, this phenomenon will play a role in the very survival of mankind. Well, I admit that might be a reach.

Luckily, while Kouba was helping out on the move, he stumbled across a garage sale and picked up a dandy oversized bird cage. No one seemed to know how the bird had grown to be this large, but Augie was happy with his new digs, and it stopped the irritating and continuous noisy head bumping at night.

* * *

A welcoming party for Graham was planned, and it was understood that quite a few ladies would attend. Kouba Kenta scored some top-shelf "whacker pot" for the party. This was the first-time meeting for Graham Reginald McNichols and Lucinda May Obermeyer. The party was a smash hit, with great food, a really hot band, fabulous weed and the chance meeting with Lucinda. Graham thought she was a knockout and couldn't keep his eyes off her.

They finally got close enough to chit-chat about the obligatory stuff we all seem to talk about in our society. That, of course, would be: who has divorced the most times; how many kids do you have; careers; politics; religion; hang-ups; and do you like pizza and tacos, or are organic salads and finger food more a part of your lifestyle? It's always good to get past this social banter so that one can see if there is any real potential for a meaningful relationship. Graham knew right away that he wanted to spend time with the lovely Ms. Obermeyer; he was smitten by her right from the "Hi there, I'm Lucinda. You must be the stud everybody's talking about." Graham blushed, as his head was in ding-dong mode over her direct interest in him. We think he knew she was going to be the one in his life forever at that very moment.

A few weeks passed by before they hooked up for a dinner date. Graham made reservations at the Chef Boy-O'-Boy Steakhouse and Pub. He had decided that he would let her choose the wine. (What a guy. Right?) Graham had preselected and reserved the curved booth that was elevated slightly above the other tables. The rich chestnut-colored leather couch was beautifully upholstered with tufts and pleats and very comfortable. Over the top of their gazebo-styled cubicle was a trellis formed into a dome-shape enclosure laced with creeping vines that were loaded with honeysuckle and wisteria and bunches of nasturtiums.

The couple began with the finest of gourmet appetizers and a carafe of exceptional merlot wine. The Italian sausages were stuffed with cream cheese, rolled in ground paprika and garnished with finely chopped cilantro and minced garlic. For her main entrée, Lucinda chose the "Spiegnatte" spiral spaghetti with truffles in organic green tomato pepper sauce. Graham, showing he was a man's man, ordered the 16-ounce porterhouse aged beefsteak; it would be served with coriander and seared to perfection with a bright hot pink center, just a hair shy of the classic medium-rare. The Chef Boy-O'-Boy steaks were always cooled to 40 degrees Fahrenheit, basted in lemon-pepper sprinkle and sea salt, then sizzle-grilled over a stainless steel barbecue unit that was custom-built by Sears, the one and only Model 640b. With the steak, he chose chopped garlic cloves crushed into the mashed potatoes. The garnish was a medley of finely sliced beets, carrots and green onion and a master's sprinkling of golden olive oil blended with cannabis-infused butter.

Both meals were served with a simple green salad topped with chopped cilantro and an Italian dressing drawn from some secret old family creation. Their dinners were delivered in grand style by both the owners, Dino and Luigi. At Graham's earlier request, they wore their tuxedos for this special occasion, along with diamond stickpins in their starched white serving bibs, and shiny black patent leather shoes. Their thick Sicilian black hair was slicked back with Jerris brand hair oil and tonic. Only a few patrons were ever offered this much attention.

Violins and cellos lifted the air into romantic musical interludes and sweeping flourishes, cascading as if in a gentle waterfall... Awww. It was pure restaurant drama with the precision of a Russian ballet, all in a setting of soft blue lighting. (Maynard was moved to tears.)

Graham and Lucinda ate slowly and precisely. They carefully balanced the remaining individual portions as they enjoyed this delicious and flawless presentation with royal style and grace, confidently showing their obvious training in the art of fine gourmet dining. They moved on to their second bottle of Beaujolais Napoléon #942 (575 bucks a pop). On the way to their booth for desert was a flaming chocolate éclair covered with a special dark liqueur that was served in a limited amount, and only to the finest patrons. It had been produced in Sicily for many years by Dino's family and supposedly sold exclusively to Mafia Dons. It was said to be a favorite of the infamous Godfather, Don Corleone. (Both Marlon and Maynard agreed.)

Their dinner conversation was comfortable, interesting and sometimes humorous, with

Lucinda being the one to carry most of the energy throughout the evening. Graham wanted it that way. There was still some sketchy little thing about her that he couldn't quite put his finger on.

They adjourned to the upstairs balcony and took in the expansive view of the magnificent Morello Valley. There was a gentle breeze, and the full moon gave the evening a soft light, with depth and shadowy colors. Graham looked into Lucinda's eyes, then gently but firmly pulled her to his chest and whispered, "I am going to marry you, and sooner is better than later."

Lucinda May, with a hint of hesitation, responded by lowering her beautiful eyelashes over her "China doll" complexion and said, "I will think on it tonight, but for now I must address the call of nature, for the red wine has spoken to me in rolling, tinkling, thunderous motions." Graham laughed and was pleased with her wit and sense of humor. Bravo and kudos to the Beaujolais Napoléon #942.

Well, Graham waited a very long time for Lucinda to return to the balcony. Suddenly he knew he must go look for her. He had a bad feeling about the amount of time that had elapsed, but mostly a concern about whether or not she was okay. He met both Dino and Luigi downstairs; the look on their faces said it all. The *Commendatores* shrugged with a sigh and reported to Graham what they knew. "She simply said she was called away and that you knew about it — she would be in touch with you later."

Graham began to experience a brain vibration of monumental size and disbelief. He, of course, had no idea that Lucinda suffered from multiple personality disorder. It would be years and one child later before he knew the truth.

* * *

Lucinda had no control over her affliction. One of her personalities was a character named Dottie Monet who was criminally insane and robbed banks along with savings and loan companies. Another one of her "selves" was a concert pianist internationally known as Nelda Zaffely, presumably of Polish descent. She even had a professional travel and booking agent with an agenda of concert dates for her, including world-class appearances in London, Paris, Rome, Los Angeles, San Francisco, Moscow, Hong Kong, Washington, DC, Toronto, and her favorite, Carnegie Hall in New York City. She also played in other symphony halls and performed minor concerts across the country.

She would drop out of her normal Lucinda May Obermeyer life for extensive periods. While away, she would just magically appear in the concert world as Nelda Zaffely. She was a master of disguise and had everyone fooled. She had no clue herself, as it was the illness that was running the show.

Over the ensuing years, Graham would often go nuts trying to find her; sometimes she would drop out for months.

When in her criminal mode as Dottie Monet, she would plan and carry out some very serious bank robberies and, just for the fun of it, knock off a few savings and loan companies as well; they were so easy it was laughable. Dottie always selected her black pussycat costume with the tall pointy ears, long cat whiskers and a swishy tail with a white tip on the end. She wore three-fingered gloves over her paws.

One of her fun things to do during a particular heist was to have all the bank employees, along with any customers who might be there, strip down to their underwear. She would line them up and march them right into the bank's vault. Next she would call several pizza joints and order six large pepperoni-and-mushroom combos and two gallons of root beer from each of them to be delivered to the bank, supposedly for a company party. She always left in the nick of time with bags full of cash.

News of her capers spread internationally, and she somehow became a cult hero and developed a huge fan base, who adopted "Go get 'em, Dottie — *meow-meow*" as their mantra. Black cat costumes were soon bestsellers in variety stores everywhere. Yep, from Target to Neiman Marcus and Walmart to Nordstrom. They even had them in kiddie sizes. A retail success story was unfolding at its very best. *Meow-meow.*

Dottie would return home to Rushtuk and become Lucinda May Obermeyer again as if nothing had happened. As far as she knew, it was the truth. Clinically, this phenomenon is sometimes called "the convenient sensory brain block." What was always truly amazing was her ability to come up with logical and believable explanations to family and friends for her absence.

* * *

When Lucinda finally reappeared in his life a few weeks after their first date at Chef Boy-O'-Boy, Graham was so happy to have her back that he got over her unexplained disappearance and didn't get around to asking her any serious questions. The subject of marriage came up several times. Graham finally said, "I want to give you a big fancy wedding with all the trimmings."

Lucinda responded, "That would be great," and once again lowered those long lovely eyelashes down over her China doll complexion. She squeezed Graham's hand, hesitated, then let him know that she had another plan. "I have a better idea — let's elope."

They did exactly that, as the two of them caught the next flight to Tahiti, with no hesitation or discussion. They spent two weeks island hopping and being very much in love.

* * *

Once Graham and Lucinda May were back in Rushtuk, things went smoothly at first. Several months passed and Graham's grooming for a career in government was successful; he became a State Senator with substantial powers. Lucinda was the happiest she had ever been and orchestrated the design and construction of a rustic but beautiful ranch-style log cabin and large hay barn for their home life.

However, after several months, her illness once again showed signs of reappearing. Lucinda May realized that there was nothing she could do about it. She never knew just who might be the next character to take over her life, but there was never more than one personality at a time.

It was the second of July and three days before Lucinda's birthday. Graham planned a surprise party and invited all their friends to a huge community barbecue. He found the original band that had played the first night they met, and he persuaded them to come and join in. Lucinda had been busy secretly packing concert dresses; and should it be bank-robbing duty again, she had the black pussycat outfit tucked in as well. All of this preparation was done while she was in the pre-trance state of mind, which never left her with a memory. It always preceded the inevitable personality change. She was sad and somber, for she did not want to leave.

Before the party really got started, Lucinda began morphing into the personality of "Dottie Monet," the notorious bank robber. Then she simply vanished before the band started to play. Graham was so busy attending to the hundreds of guests, friends and celebrities that he didn't notice her absence right away.

* * *

Lucinda's newest trip outside normal reality would end up with a rather huge surprise. After being gone for nearly a year and knocking off five regular banks and three savings and loan firms, she returned home with a beautiful four-month-old baby girl, whom she had named Gracie Aylene McNichols. This gorgeous child had Lucinda's blond hair and knuckle-deep dimples; her eyes were a royal blue, just like Graham's. She also had his perpetually tan skin color. Gracie was a picture of health and showed early signs of alertness and self-awareness. She giggled and wiggled and could already crawl quite well, exploring everything in sight. Clearly, she was unique, special and destined to have an amazing life.

Gracie had knowledge far beyond her days of being here on this planet. You could sense it when she observed people: there was a look of purpose, a look of understanding, a look of knowing the future. She just had to wait until her body — or, as she later referred to it, her "bio vessel" — matured into its genetically programmed full potential. Kouba

Kenta Bailey became her mentor and life coach. He knew that she would have extraordinary powers.

Upon seeing this infant, Graham, being mostly speechless, could only say, "How could all of this have happened?" Lucinda's response was a heavily paused shoulder shrug, after which she answered, "I dunno — beats the heck out of me," and said no more. Graham, at a later date, did secretly get a paternity test, and yep, Gracie Aylene was his, alright.

Graham had long ago learned not to press for too much information. He was just happy to have Lucinda back, as he loved her deeply. His affection for Gracie, who was becoming even more beautiful every day, simply grew and grew. Graham became the best ever at being a father. Lucinda was thrilled; she was still in love with her mate and settled back into the role of homemaker, and now doting mom as well. She was really good at it.

Chapter Two

Gracie Struts Her Stuff

Several years had now passed. Graham was still the Senator from Idaho and was very popular. He was being looked at by the power hacks from Washington, DC, with classic greedy political eyes. He would not be swayed, as he was not corruptible; besides, he was perfectly happy serving the citizens of Idaho and living the dream life at home.

I also need to mention that there had been no arrests yet in all those bank robberies. The police did not even have the slightest clue... Hmmm. Graham, for whatever reason, never mentioned to anyone that he had found several laundry sacks stuffed with cash in the loft out in the barn — so much cash he couldn't count all of it.

Young Gracie knew the sacks were there but said nothing, either. She enjoyed doing other things while hanging out in the loft. She always liked to take out "Nelda's" concert gowns and try them on and look at herself in the large, cracked, floor-to-ceiling mirror with the beautiful mahogany frame. It was stored next to the old beat-up steamer trunk. She also loved trying on the black pussycat costume and prancing around while practising her interpretations of meows, cat purring and swiping strategically at the death's-head hawk moths in the air. They are also known as *Acherontia atropos* moths. (Maynard has a collection of them mounted in a wooden box under a tinted glass lid.)

Eventually, Graham knew it was time to face the reality of the cash being there; it would not be good if this secret leaked out to the wrong, and very possibly dangerous, people. He had to protect his family at all costs. He decided to share this revelation with Kouba Kenta Bailey, his buddy in arms. Graham knew that Gracie was becoming old enough to want to know what the heck all that money was doing in the loft. As for Gracie, she just didn't want the barn rats to eat it all up. Old calico pussycat Spike had been falling down on the job of catching the little buggers, anyway. He simply wanted to catch Augie McFarland, the parakeet — for him, it was personal.

Gracie liked having Kouba Kenta Bailey around, as he made her laugh a lot and he fixed really good sandwiches. He would also take her for some very scary rides on the Vespa. He never really got the hang of it, and he didn't know how to slow down for sharp corners. I'm guessing they were just lucky, however, as we all found out later that Gracie had special and powerful abilities to control many things, including gravity, musical tones and various shades of color. That is how we came to understand why they never crashed. She loved their friendship and called him "Uncle KK." She was also just fine with his occasional display of the chicken-leg-bone-through-the-lip-under-the-nose routine.

* * *

To elaborate on his background, Kouba Kenta Bailey was born George Alfred Bailey in London, England, to a white father living in both the UK and Nigeria. George's father had married his African childhood friend — and, by the way, a first cousin — who was black. Apparently, the Baileys had some kind of ancestry connecting them to the British royal family. (It was rumored that the Queen often had tea and crumpets with Kouba's Nigerian mother.)

George was healthy in every respect; what made him exceptional was the fact that he was an albino with soft pink eyes, pure white wavy hair and long Rasta dreadlocks. His father worked for MI6, which is Britain's secret service arm of the government, similar to the American CIA. Members were licensed to kill if necessary. Just like Bond... "James Bond." (Maynard winces and rolls his eyes.) His parents didn't know it yet, but George A. Bailey was also very smart, with an IQ that would be off the charts. He later became savant-like when it came to problem solving and forecasting.

The British government would be lucky to have him. When George was only 13, he was sent on a secret 007-type mission to Nigeria, with approval from his parents. He was to gather information on a presumed overthrow of the current regime, which was controlled by the Crown. They all knew that it would be a high-risk but very important undertaking. Unfortunately, soon after arriving, young George was kidnapped and held prisoner by a tribe of insane and hairless Ubangi tribesmen who lived deep in the African jungle.

These warriors had never seen an albino before and felt sure he must have magical powers. He was smart enough to go along with this and demanded that they do certain things for him, or he would threaten them with terrible illnesses and cause them to experience the dreaded shriveling tongue and swollen eyeball disease.

To further keep them in line, George would also show off his powers by beating them at playing checkers, pinching rocks, tossing horseshoes and doing card tricks. (Maynard wants it to be noted that not one of you readers has questioned just how horseshoes were being found in the deepest part of the African jungle.)

The Ubangi women demanded that their men listen to and obey the young Bailey. He was treated like a god, and they even bestowed the African name Kouba Kenta, which honoured him with great status.

Ten years later, at age 23, Kouba managed to escape his Ubangi captors and caught an ocean freighter to San Francisco, where he would soon meet Graham McNichols. Graham liked him right off the bat but wasn't sure that the chicken bone under the nose was going to fly, even in San Francisco. Perhaps it just might in the Haight-Ashbury district, which was always full of weird folks and strange stuff.

Only a few would even notice, given the level of daily drug use.

Quite often after his arrival, Kouba would hear someone holler out, "Hey, where can I get me one of them lip bones?" He would smile and tell them to go over to Miranda's Chicken Bone Shop on Lombard Street. The response was either "Okay," or "Really?"

* * *

Gracie excelled in school and in her relationships with adults and with her own peer group. She had fully inherited her mother's good looks, and her musical talents as well. That was obviously strange, since the only time Lucinda could play a single note was when she was in character as Nelda Zaffely. Gracie was the only one, apart from Kouba, who knew about Lucinda's incredible secrets, and she kept the truth to herself. She loved her mother and watched over her by using her extraordinary powers.

Uncle KK knew of Gracie's abilities because of his own unique arrangement with the universe. He drew heavily on his mystical knowledge gained while living with the Ubangi. Kouba Kenta knew of the many separate and different realities available to those who could connect with them, including those experienced by Lucinda. Gracie and KK could both hear starbursts, smell rainbows, collect dreams of dark chocolate and breathe in the vibrations of all music. Kouba could always find some really good cannabis, as well.

As Gracie continued to mature, she began to get a better grasp on what she could do with her own special and dynamic powers. She learned what was available to her and when, as there is always a controlling power over all those blessed in this truly divine manner. It is a requirement that the gift be used for good. To abuse these powers would result in losing them, and the abuser would have to walk on the streets of shame forever.

Kouba Kenta Bailey assisted Gracie in learning the appropriate uses of the gifts that were specifically assigned to and for her alone. At age 16 she was already a raging beauty with a "glow in the dark" presence about her. Gracie's aura shimmered whenever the natural light started to fade. She had to be careful and not let it get too bright, as people would notice and ask questions.

* * *

Well, when it comes to kids, ya gotta know that sometimes 16-year-olds just have to show off, right? Our Gracie was no exception. Late one summer afternoon, while the family was on vacation, Gracie attended the outdoor concert in the redwoods near Mendocino, California. The Sequoia Symphony Orchestra was performing its annual fall concert. This was always the biggest social event of the year, with hundreds or possibly thousands of classical music lovers sitting on the beautifully manicured grounds and facing a large stage fashioned in a shape identical to the Hollywood Bowl amphitheater near Los Angeles. The symphony orchestra boasted a playing membership of 138 musicians and two internationally celebrated conductors.

The weather was perfect — warm, with lots of sunshine and a gentle onshore breeze from the teal-blue Pacific Ocean. There were the occasional sweet, smoky wafts of the ages-old and historic Humboldt County green and gold cannabis buds, naturally laced with reddish hair strands. The smoke from the weed floated in and out all day long, like waves swirling through the air.

Gracie Aylene McNichols felt like showing off a little bit, so when intermission commenced, she climbed up onto the stage, which was now cleared of musicians, and proceeded to skip across it just like any certified teenybopper would do in front of the crowd. The festival patrons were polite and reacted with a curious but enthusiastic applause. She was wearing a dress featuring multicoloured butterfly prints on a white background and a classic Peter Pan collar with eyelet trim. Around her waist was a wide, pleated red satin sash. White ankle socks and vintage-style black Mary Jane shoes completed her outfit. Gracie's longish hair was styled in layers of blond curls. She was obviously destined to be a lifelong fashion buff.

To the amazement and concern of concert-goers and the security personnel, Gracie noticed two or three startled uniformed policemen who were moving towards her, no doubt to escort her off the stage and to someplace else. Without warning, she suddenly spun around on her heels, blinked three times and pointed her two index fingers like a gun fighter while she tossed up one black Mary Jane shoe at them. After a giggle and a wiggle of her ears, she stopped the security guards right in their tracks with a single white laser-like cosmic zap. (Maynard mused, "Oh — Vo-Dee-Oh – Doe-Doe-Doe." Thanks, Laverne; thanks, Shirley.)

Gracie found chairs for the cops, sat them down and instructed them to be quiet and listen while she played. For whatever reason, they nodded and agreed. Everybody else, having been put on "life pause," just watched with the classic "deer in the headlights" expression. Gracie was near the middle of the stage, where there was an old wooden musical relic from the distant past. Turns out that it was the remnants of an ancient upright piano leaning with a noticeable warp to its frame; it had been abandoned there long ago. History tells us that the piano was used for eons in one of Humboldt County's honky-tonk Western bars. It was a tired old rickety-tickety piano, for sure.

Gracie sat down on a seat that had the classic velvet jungle-animal print covering the cushion. She placed her outstretched palms face down on the carved wooden panel that was in front of the strings and the wool-felt-covered strike hammers that were situated right above the stained and chipped ivory piano keys. She blinked three times and once again wiggled her ears, then giggled with that mile-wide smile of hers. The piano vibrated into a clouded technicolor swirl and seemed to come to life all on its own. The strings were cleaned, tightened and tuned in an instant. The keys, both black and white, realigned and responded to her perfect touch. The wood creaked, groaned and straightened. The floor pedals no longer squeaked due to too much dirt and spilled beer over decades of neglect.

All of this was accomplished in a matter of seconds. The piano had been entirely refreshed. That didn't matter much, because Gracie had the entire crowd on sensory lockdown, anyway. They weren't going anywhere until Gracie Aylene McNichols decided they could go. They were gathered there to hear her special piano recital, and that was it.

Gracie, thanks to her special powers, could take any inanimate object such as this honky-tonk cowboy piano and give it, well, a life presence of its own. It appeared to have warmth and a conscious understanding of what was soon to take place. The piano somehow knew that it was about to express to the concert-goers sounds they neither expected nor had ever heard. It would be a once-in-a-lifetime experience for the crowd to hear and feel cosmic music in dual tones with multiple crescendos, along with the magical moments of colors cascading from the edge of the amphitheater. This would be in accordance with the perfect sounds emanating from the fresh slick pine varnish. Suddenly, once ready, she released her hold on the crowd of classical music lovers; this put them back into their normal reality. (Maynard was speechless.)

Gracie Aylene McNichols

Gracie waited for total quiet, and just at the right moment she began to play shortened versions of the three most popular compositions by Wolfgang Amadeus Mozart. Then, with a flourish and a silent, double-wristed "phrasing" motion, she moved quickly on to composer Sergei Rachmaninoff and the "Black Prince" refrain, before continuing with Strauss's "Opus 4," Chopin's "Nocturne in B Flat Major" and Beethoven's "Paris Interlude" concerto. Needless to say, the crowd was stunned and loved the momentum that was being generated. They were entertained in a way never imagined by anyone. It was pure magic.

As Gracie looked around the stage, she noticed that all the members of the orchestra had quietly taken their seats and that both conductors had moved to center stage. They were poised and focused, awaiting her command. With more unexplained wizardry, several printed sheets of music suddenly appeared in front of each of the musicians.

Gracie then totally transformed the flavor of the concert and continued with a spectacular collection of classic rock 'n' roll songs that went something like this: Led Zeppelin's "Stairway to Heaven," Rod Stewart's "Forever Young," Foreigner's "I've Been Waiting," Phil Collins' "Just Another Day in

Paradise," John Lennon's "Imagine" and finally Pink Floyd's "Us and Them." The crowd knew all the words and sang along in a perfect passionate harmony; the blend of the voices with Gracie's piano playing and the Sequoia Symphony Orchestra was exceptional.

The powerful sounds filled the entire Mendocino landscape past Monterey, vibrating all the way down to Big Sur. The surge of music burst upward into the stars and rippled the Milky Way. This caused an unexpected interruption of a celestial moment in time. Astronomers worldwide were flabbergasted; even the atomic clocks, which measure the rotation of our planet, had to be reset. They had no idea what had just happened. It was later rumored that from their heavenly distant strands of consciousness, Albert Einstein and Stephen Hawking had both tossed in a couple of eye blinks while in their very deep sleep. The vibrations came from their own separate realities. Well, e certainly equals good ol' mc squared, doesn't it? Or perhaps oblonged? It would all be debated for years to come. (Maynard was filled with silly purple plums of ecstasy.)

A shimmering full moon appeared low in the horizon, expressing a never-seen-before shade of orange. It seemed to be pulsing over the ocean in a serpentine motion as it moved slowly through the night, occasionally tossing moonbeams down onto the stage and into the crowd. Timothy Leary and his buddy Ram Dass would have been proud.

Gracie rose from the gnarled old beer-stained honky-tonk piano with a loving smile on her face. She took a simple bow and threw a kiss to all in the audience as the musicians quietly stood in awe, many with tears streaming down their faces. Time seemed to just drift in and out of this surreal and special occasion. Sadly, no one who was there would have an actual memory of what had really happened in this beautiful magical place known as Mendocino. (It's okay to cry, Maynard — it's okay.)

Kouba Kenta Bailey was upset with Gracie's antics at the Sequoia Symphony Orchestra concert and advised her to never do that again. "It's too risky," he said. "Only you and I and a few others know of your powers. The masses are simply not ready for this kind of experience and exposure. Look what happened to JC, for goodness sake." (Maynard says it could also be "for Christ's sake," but we won't debate that for now.)

Gracie promised to turn down the knobs on the visual fantasies and only do small miracles from now on. Uncle KK knew better, so he decided that he would definitely have to monitor her more closely. Secretly, he grinned at all of it and actually thought that her performance was fabulous.

Gracie Aylene put the crowd on cosmic hold once again as she floated away, taking their concert memories and dreams with her, and then *poof,* she vanished into the sky, heading over to the Arizona desert to visit the Silver Fox, the one with the emerald-green eyes. He had been waiting for her.

Chapter Three

Dottie Monet Solves a Pizza Crisis, Meow-Meow

A few months had passed. The Senator — that would be Graham Reginald McNichols, Gracie's dad — was once again trying to locate his wife, Lucinda. He wanted to discuss Gracie's going off to university even though she was only 16 years old. He tried the neighbors and the Internet and of course called all of their friends. No luck, but he did notice all the news about the rash of bank and savings and loan robberies.

It seemed that the fairy-tale celebrity bank bandit was in full force, wearing the black pussycat costume with the pointy ears, the cat whiskers and the long tail with a white tip. Once again, Dottie was holding up the money changers all over Idaho, Washington State and even the provinces of British Columbia and Alberta. She was way up there in that place known as Canada. Eh? Dottie kept the Canadian cash in a separate sack just so she could show respect and be politically correct.

She was an international hit once more. Even the nighttime TV shows were picking up on it and writing comedy skits. They were getting movie stars to play "Dottie Monet" in the pussycat outfits. Wannabe actors were showing up in their underwear, hoping to get hired on as extras to be tossed into the bank vaults with the employees. The TV audiences would faithfully chant the mantra "Go get 'em, Dottie — *meow-meow*." She was just a-robbing those banks clean as a whistle. Yep, our gal was still a-stuffing those employees and customers into the vaults while stripping them down to their underwear. They, of course, kept the pizza and root beer coming.

Okay, time out — somebody somewhere is going to be smart enough to make a movie out of this; it's only a matter of time. Perhaps it will happen after this unknown author wins the coveted Pulitzer Prize for best new and original comedy. What? You say it couldn't happen? Maybe, or maybe not. Who really knows for sure? (Maynard says, "You just keep on a-dreaming there, cowboy.")

Anyway, during her latest robbery, Dottie called and ordered the usual pizza combo takeout as a courtesy. It was reported that on this heist, a Danny DeVito look-alike delivered the pizza, root beer and plenty of napkins. Dottie said that Danny needed to go into the vault as well. There was loads of pizza — it was all good.

She often invited guys and gals from the local fire departments as well. Dottie always waved goodbye to them with a classic Queen Elizabeth side-to-side hand motion, giving out three or four meows and a loud purr.

The media was having a field day. With all the TV attention from the celebrity talk show hosts, it was "Lights! Camera! Action!" She was breaking all the news snippets and nuggets as her cult status went off the popularity charts again. Dottie Monet pussycat tee-shirts and costumes were selling in the thousands of units and at an unprecedented rate. Also, it seemed as though every other car and pickup truck you saw on the freeways had a "*Meow-meow*" or "Go get 'em, Dottie" bumper sticker on it. She was in rock star mode, for sure. (Maynard wasn't certain, but someone said that a sticker was seen on the back of a Polish submarine.)

The Senator had no way of knowing what the heck was happening, and of course Kouba Kenta Bailey was clearly suspicious, but our Gracie knew full well all along who it was, and she would handle it when the time was right.

Several more large bags of cash were headed for the barn to be tossed up into the loft.

It was inevitable that sooner or later "Dottie" would be caught. It happened one Friday afternoon during a bank caper in downtown Boise. Everything was going normally; she had just washed the pussycat costume and it was fluffy and shone with a brushed-up sparkle. The bank heist was slick and orderly, and the vault was as usual packed with people in the normally abnormal way. Those who had heard of her were thrilled to be there, as it gave them their moment in history. Great stuff for telling the grandkids.

When the pizza arrived, it was cold. Dottie was really teed off and called the pizza joint to complain and give 'em the dickens for sending out subpar pizza: there was not nearly enough cheese, and the sauce was watery and tasteless as well. Chewing the crust was like biting off a piece of tractor tire rubber. The pepperoni was as hard as a child's large-size winter coat button or a one-inch flat metal washer. Also, the root beer was totally off, with no fizz at all and not cold. No one likes warm root beer, even if it does have a fizz to it.

The assistant manager said he would offer them a credit, but he had to wait for an approval from Pizza Corporate Inc. and they were in Atlanta, Georgia, which is in a different time zone, so they were probably closed. The board members were no doubt in a bar or on the golf course somewhere. Dottie told him that he had better straighten this out or she would go over to the pizza joint and scratch his eyes out, *meow-meow!*

The folks in the bank's vault cheered and said, "You go get 'em, Dottie!" Well, her heart was in the right place, for sure, but she took too much time and the cops nabbed her.

In the patrol car on her way to jail, Dottie was heard to say, "Darn it, I knew I should have ordered tacos, or at least chips and salsa, instead." There was one thing she was totally right about; the quality of pizza was way off the mark almost everywhere, especially the home or office delivery.

Kouba Kenta Bailey had been having meetings with Dino and Luigi at the Chef Boy-O'-Boy Steakhouse and Pub about this very issue. They decided to call and file a complaint with the local pizza police. Graham said he would use his political powers to see that this was handled right away. He thought it would also be a good way to kick off his run for higher office. He was encouraged by his wife, Lucinda May, along with Kouba and Gracie Aylene.

Wouldn't you know it — right off the bat, Graham shot for the top job, and bingo, just like that, he reached out and caught the brass ring and was voted in as Idaho's new "United States Senator." He was perfect for the job; Graham could charm the sparkle out of a silver-winged fairy's wand with a blink and a wink and leave her with her knees knocking out a well-known Buddy Rich drum solo. (Maynard encourages all of you to look up Buddy Rich online.)

Committees were formed and plans were made. Graham wanted the community of Rushtuk to blossom. Kouba Kenta Bailey was to be Master of Ceremonies at the victory dinner. Just for laughs, Kenta wore one of the outfits made for him while he was being held captive in the jungles of Africa by the Ubangi tribe. He slapped in a brand new "latest fashion" chrome-plated chicken leg bone through his upper lip right there under his nose.

The crowd just loved it — especially his custom-fit real leopard skin bodysuit complete with long tail. He had a headdress made from birds of paradise flowers, which fit in nicely with his wavy Rasta-styled pure white hair, including the massive, now two-foot-long dreadlocks. This entire mess was rearranged into a spectacular multicolored headdress with an assortment of long turkey feathers.

Later that evening, Graham and Kouba Kenta Bailey went over to cut a deal with Dino and Luigi, the owners of the Chef Boy-O'-Boy Steakhouse and Pub, for a licence to grow several varieties of cannabis when it became legal, which was coming up very soon. Graham was going to be in charge of making decisions on who was gonna get really rich, really fast. Hmmm. The brothers already had a large greenhouse, and it would be simple to convert the building for growing massive quantities of high-grade "whacker weed." Dino and Luigi would think on it; they wondered what Graham wanted in return. Double hmmm!

Chapter Four

Lucinda Sees a Shrink

The court date for Lucinda, a.k.a. Dottie Monet, came and went. The review of the bank robbery charges was put on hold, and she was free to go home and be with Graham and Gracie. Judge Aaron K. Ledbetter didn't quite know what to do; should he charge her as Lucinda May Obermeyer McNichols, or as Dottie Monet? The judge was also, of course, Graham's golfing buddy. Needless to say, we had a problem here. Finally, it was decided to let the local psychiatrist, Dr. Hal Hankerbee, deal with the situation, as long as most of the loot was returned. (Uh-huh. We're not sure what Maynard thinks yet.)

Graham knew where the cash was. There were bags and bags of it up in the loft out in the hay barn. He decided to keep it safe for the banks. (Oh yeah, sure... "You betchum, Red Ryder," said Little Beaver.) He could then decide what to do with it later. Kouba Kenta Bailey thought he should dole it out to charities, as the banks had robbery insurance and would be covered, anyway.

Unbeknownst to both Kouba and Graham, our little Miss Gracie had also discovered the bags of cash way back when she turned 12 and had enjoyed a great birthday party. She often played for hours in the loft, training homing pigeons, eating yucca dust cookies and dancing with moonbeams as they darted down through the cracks in the barn's roof. Gracie didn't care much about the bags of money, as she had plenty of cash whenever needed. She was pretty sure that her mom was the culprit and that she was not only Nelda Zaffely but Dottie Monet as well. Gracie had learned to make the distinction, which wasn't hard to do. Years earlier she had discovered the old steamer trunk with the costumes, all the beautiful concert gowns and of course the black pussycat outfit. Gracie also knew that Nelda Zaffely was in fact the concert pianist who had morphed from Lucinda as well.

Oh, by the way, ever since Nelda had vanished, the concert promoters were going nuts trying to locate her. They were facing financial ruin, as the concert tickets had sold out in all of the venues. Millions of dollars would have to be refunded should she not be found. Given that this was an international problem, Interpol and other search groups worked day and night trying to find her. The promoters were so desperate that one corporate brainiac suggested using a fake lookalike double who could play as well as Nelda, and just getting on with it. The idea was gaining traction. (Maynard thought they probably could have something here.)

Only this tireless writer, yours truly, had figured out that Gracie might be the solution, as she was even better at the piano than Nelda was. Great scam here, folks — stay tuned. ("You betchum, Red Ryder.")

Meanwhile, Kouba Kenta and Gracie Aylene were spending hours in the loft practising the art of levitation and fine-tuning her other gifts, which were the sole possession of this very special child.

* * *

Dr. Hal Hankerbee was in full control of Lucinda's future at this point. He didn't see any reason for her to have to go to prison; no one had been hurt in all of her escapades, and he was very excited to have the opportunity to study this strange condition that affected so few people. His ego was in full-throttle mode as he thought about how famous he was going to be when and if he solved the mysteries of Lucinda's multiple personality disorder. He was evil enough and also prepared to keep and control her freedoms as long as he wanted to. All legally, of course. Boy, was he in for a surprise.

Lucinda didn't have any idea what all of this was about; how could she — she had no knowledge of these characters. Dottie who? Nelda who? "What the heck is going on here? I'm going home," Lucinda said at the end of the afternoon. Well, the armed guard was always there to see that she stayed until Graham picked her up. The paranoia was really starting to set in with her.

Graham realized that he needed help. Fortunately, KK Bailey was going to save the day, with Gracie's assistance. They would take an anticipatory lap on the Vespa just for good luck.

Lucinda wondered if someone was planning something wicked and sinister, such as going after the Obermeyer fortunes. The oil business was astronomical, and there were also the massive holdings in the forestry leases in the Pacific Northwest, as well as the potential land development. The lumber alone was worth billions. Lucinda was the only legal heir to all of this. Graham wasn't even aware of how huge this inheritance really was. Gracie knew to the penny how much it was worth, even at the tender age of nearly 17. She didn't really care, either. Because of her relationship with Kouba Kenta Bailey, her life was filled with cosmic powers, and together they planned many adventures which would affect the lives, hopes and dreams of a chosen few.

Grace would not allow Dr. Hal Hankerbee to harm her mother. So she had several pranks put together to keep this phoney-baloney shrink in line. She decided to really mess with Dr. Hank's head; for example, when he got up to go to work in the morning, he would often find out that all of his shoes had shrunk. They were at least two sizes too small and pinched his feet. His suits were three sizes too large, making him look like a bozo goofball country hick. Spunky Grace also lengthened his neckties by about 10 or 11 inches. When he would make phone calls, any and everyone who answered spoke only Navajo or Swahili. She would hide his car keys at least once a week; sometimes she would hide his car as well, after running it down and killing off its battery. Did I mention the occasional flat tires?

Our Gracie was able to do all this through her awesome powers and what seemed like divine control over the systemic molecular motions in nature. She would move the significant elements of Hankerbee's reality into the sidereal moments of a fortnight. Once, she moved his entire house over to the vacant lot across the street. After he went to report it, he came back and found it to be right where it should be, only facing in the opposite direction. In other words, his front porch was now his back porch. He was smart enough not to tell too many of his associates about all the strange things going on in his life. Maybe he just needed a vacation. Ha! Did I mention that Gracie had also turned him into a compulsive serial adult bedwetter?

* * *

One day, while Lucinda was in therapy, Dr. Hal excused himself to take a phone call outside his office. He said that he would only be a minute. Lucinda flipped open a file on his desk and suddenly realized why she was really there. The papers were documents pertaining to case histories of patients who had been diagnosed with multiple personality disorder. She smelled a rat! She would have to play it coy and appear to be very interested in the process.

At around the same time, Lucinda was also getting the familiar vibrations that preceded her personality changes. This time it was quite different; the sensations were more intense, deeper, and yet calm in another way. She knew that something was going to happen — but just didn't know when. She also was aware that there was nothing she could do about it. For sure, though, she knew that it would not be Nelda or Dottie this time.

Lucinda decided to start reading up on this strange condition of hers, as it was only a matter of time before the new personality took over. The power surges in her brain were growing almost daily. She realized that she needed to share all of these experiences with Gracie Aylene. She felt guilty and was concerned that her daughter would not understand the depth of this highly unusual predicament.

Nonetheless, Gracie welcomed the chance to help her mom, as she had quite a story of her own to tell. The bond between the two of them was an experience few of us will ever get to know. It was all about trust, respect and love. This would be an opportunity for her to reveal herself to Lucinda and express some of her powers, as well as explain how it all came to be.

Gracie appeared out of nowhere and said, "Come with me to the barn — we'll go up into the loft, where I'll show you something that I think you need to know about." It was autumn and nearly dusk; the wispy buttermilk skies were sinking deep into the horizon and creating an atmosphere of warmth, serenity and peacefulness.

* * *

It has been brought to the attention of the writer that no information has been offered up yet as to how it was that Gracie Aylene McNichols had all this cosmic power. Actually, it's quite complicated in its structure but simple to understand at the same time. Basically, it has to do with the compliance of all of the separate and universal configurations that must follow the natural order of physical motion. As there is no end to space, we all know that grand movements of measurable masses of matter are continually expanding and obeying the connected laws of gravity.

This is due to the pressures being created when at least two floating and growing star groups form and then touch or outright slam into each other. Colossal eruptions and cataclysmic explosions cause formations of gas-filled bodies of space sparklers that are shaped like orbs. They, of course, undulate to the tune of crashing molecules and atoms. Some of them become attached to comets that race through different realities only to return and sometimes reach our planet. Many scientists think that it's a natural phenomenon. Mystics and other people of knowledge say that it is purpose-driven and caused by a higher power, therefore having a special preordained agenda. Crystal-like bundles of star stuff streak through our skies, striking both animate and inanimate objects. When contact is made, the components of the space globules are absorbed and either become neutralized or, conversely, should they strike a human form, often become energized as they align with the chemical vibrations in the brain. In rare cases, humans are transformed into beings having special powers. That's because our brain is in and of itself an electrochemical device of a special cellular composition. This was the case with Gracie Aylene McNichols.

It seems that on a camping trip in the wilderness of Idaho's Black Mountain Range, a globule of star stuff enveloped Gracie when she had wandered away from the campsite. She was just a toddler back then. After hours of searching and much anxiety on the part of her parents, she simply walked back into the campground and said, "Gracie hungry — I want hottie dog, Fritos chips and soda pop... NOW!!"

Gracie Aylene was forever changed. A few of the adults couldn't help but notice that she had a glow about her that was quite different from everyone else. Little did they know, however, that she was in complete control of the campsite's environment. I hope this explanation helps you, the reader, to have a better understanding of the facts. (Just want the facts, Maynard — just the facts.)

* * *

Now in the barn, Gracie spoke to her mother in a much different voice tone that did not sound familiar to Lucinda, yet it was clearly Gracie's. It was deeper, more powerful, confident, and way beyond her nearly 17 years. She had her mom sit on the hay-covered wooden planks of the loft with her legs crossed in the classic lotus meditation position. She then led Lucinda into a silent "life pause." Gracie said, "Hold my hands and breathe deeply." In less than a moment and with a wave of goosebumps for all, the entire barn took on a heavenly palette of soft pinkish colors including accents of turquoise and silver. Soft, pulsing shades of the primary waves of life sliced and danced through the cracks in the barn's rooftop and surrounded them in a warm blanket of sweet vibrations and harmonic tones. Lucinda May was physically paralyzed but calm; she felt no anxiety or fear. (Maynard says, "Yep, either one of the acid cousins Purple Microdot or Windowpane will do it almost every time.")

Magically, they both began to rise upward and off the loft's floor to a height of about five feet. There was a slight bobble and sway in the levitation, but the two of them were very stable as they floated around the air space in no particular direction. Their breathing motions joined together in a rhythm controlled by a synchronized and connected heartbeat, as if there was only one for both of them.

In her deeper voice, Gracie said to Lucinda, "Look at me, look into my eyes and see my shape. I am you, you are me. The difference in our ages does not matter. That you are my mother also does not matter. We are nothing more than simple strands of cosmic luminous 'blue light fibers.'"

You could almost hear Lucinda's brain go *crackle, boink* and *donk*. Gracie continued on, "We are love. We are sorrow. We are laughter. We are both the future and the past."

Warm vibrations suddenly embraced the moment. Outside, a gentle rain began to fall. Perfect teardrops shaped by crystals of water softly plinked and tap-danced on the old rooftop as powerful thunder could be heard in the distant and beautiful Morello Valley. There would be dramatic lightning and pulsing inside the giant cumulus thunderheads as they rolled by. Well, it was a "jumpin'-thumpin'" grand show from Mama Nature.

Gracie said to Lucinda, "You have been selected by an entity known as 'Him' to carry out this cosmic reality in a forward manner, as was I many years ago. Go and wait for his signal — he will contact you." With that, she gently lowered the two of them back to the soft hay on the loft's floor.

Then, with a great big teenage grin on her face, our normal Gracie said, "Let's go eat, I'm famished." Lucinda, not feeling too steady or quite sure of her balance, took a few steps back down the stairs to the floor of the barn and over to the main tractor room. When she turned around to see if Gracie was following, she discovered that she was alone. Gracie had simply vanished. It was confusing, to say the least, in that there was only one way out of the barn — no side door, no back door. So with another brain *crackle, boink* and *donk*, Lucinda said to herself, "Yep, I'm hungry, I'm thinking cheeseburger, yam fries and a cherry coke soda, with hot apple pie and a scoop of maple nut vanilla ice cream for desert." Silence grudgingly filled the barn.

The next morning, Lucinda looked at herself in the mirror and said, "Wow, that was one heck of a dream." Actually, she knew that it had really happened and that the experience was all true. She just wasn't prepared to deal with it yet. Suddenly the glass in her bathroom mirror began to vibrate and change its color. Surreal clouds of swirling shades of lavender appeared, along with the face of a handsome male figure. The face remained stoic and centered, making no movement whatsoever. Finally, his eyelids popped open. His eye-piercing stare was fixed in direct, targeted contact with Lucinda's very wide open facial expression. Soon the image began to fade almost as quickly as it had appeared, and a sweet voice said, "This is one place where we will meet." The entity then vanished and the mirror returned to normal. (Yes, Maynard; this is very good stuff.)

* * *

Over the following weeks and months, Lucinda vowed to try and make sense of all of this. For a while, at least, the ramblings that drove the multiple personalities in her life subsided. She was able to return to being a good mom and wife, keeping herself busy with all kinds of social projects. Dr. Hal Hankerbee was now scared to death of Lucinda and saw her as little as possible. During her last visit to his office, someone had gone over to his house, painted it bright pink and trimmed it out in neon chartreuse. The sidewalk, windows, trees and shrubs were painted as well. The neighbors had a meeting with the town council. A civic judgement was pending, and things weren't looking too bright for good ol' Dr. Hal Hankerbee. Gracie couldn't stop laughing and even got Uncle KK to see the humor in her work.

Chapter Five

Quinella Morphs from Lucinda, Meets "He, Who Is Him"

Graham, in the meantime, was busy running the people's affairs in the United States Senate for the good folks of Idaho. He didn't like being gone so much but honored his commitment to do the best he could. I have mentioned before that some of the big bosses who really ran the country and the world had been observing his work and wanted to move him up into doing their sometimes evil and often dastardly dirty deeds — you know, the stuff that always goes along with government in general.

This would entail a serious scrutiny of Graham's background, including when he lived in California. There would be an in-depth review of his family and, of course, all his friends. The kingmakers would want to know how loyal he would be to the powers that could make him very rich. Would he break the rules, could he be bought, could he keep secrets? They would have to own his very soul, for sure. The tasks they had in mind were deadly if not done exactly right. First, they would have to know if he could be trusted. When they found out about Lucinda, Gracie and Kouba Kenta Bailey, it would be interesting, no doubt.

* * *

Gracie Aylene was all excited about attending university in Pocatello that fall, even though she wouldn't be 17 until November. Not too many students were as bright as her, and Graham had certainly pulled the right strings to get her accepted. He did it the old-fashioned way; it's known as the "What do you need, and what do you want?" approach. It works almost every time. (That's what the Board of Regents is for, eh? Maynard said Graham set this one up faster than the popping sound of a forefinger-to-thumb snap.)

Grace was trying to decide what course of study to embark on. She thought it might be fine arts, including music theory and poetry. She also thought she might take a shot at nuclear quantum physics. Because of her special powers, she could do either; maybe she would do both. Gracie also liked sports and wanted to know if she could be captain of the women's volleyball team. It was approved on the spot.

Incidentally, a Dutch gal named Melinda Slipindonker had been the team's captain for the last three years and had no intention of giving it up to some daughter of a politician who had pocketbook power. She decided that making friends with Gracie would be the best way. This would give her time to find a weakness and deal little Miss Gracie Aylene some major scary grief. This Melinda person was one angry coed. However, Miss Slipindonker would be making a really stupid mistake, as Gracie was already on to her.

* * *

A few days later that fall, Lucinda's mental vibrations became stronger than they had ever been before. She knew for sure that a personalty change was imminent. She also knew that this one was different. In the past, her alternate life character would just show up. She would have no control over the change taking place or any information about who would take charge of her physical being. She never knew how long the adventure would last; as far as she was concerned, everything was normal. The big difference this time was that she was starting to get a glimpse of what, where and just who she would become.

Lucinda decided to share this strange phenomenon with Gracie and Uncle KK Bailey before she ultimately disappeared, for who knows how long this time. Would she be in any danger? The answer was yes, and she had no idea how serious the mission would be. Being asked to save the civilized world from very evil and powerful people is no small task.

The three of them decided to meet up in the loft late at night to discuss and determine some sort of strategy. Lucinda needed to figure out how to explain to Graham why, where and how long she would be gone from Idaho. She knew he would be worried sick if he wasn't sure she was safe. They needed to come up with an exit plan that was believable, and stick to it. The other problem was that the authorities would come after her as soon as they realized she was gone. This was going to take careful thinking, as no one knew or could predict her return or where she would be.

Gracie told Lucinda to visit her mirror often and wait until the lavender shades of swirling light appeared: "'He' will appear as 'Him.' Listen to his voice, and when his eyes open, focus on his stare — he will give you all that you will need to know. You will feel warmth, you will feel peace, you will experience his love and compassion. Do as he says, and you will be safe."

Both Gracie and Kouba Kenta Bailey had advance information on what was going to go down here. It was going to be super-secret, sinister and dangerous. Lucinda had been selected because of her integrity, bravery and unwavering commitment to a free society for all. Just as Lucinda was able to play piano while being Nelda Zaffely and to rob banks as Dottie Monet, she would be changed into someone else even more bizarre. Lucinda May Obermeyer McNichols was going to become fascinating and super-powerful as someone who would be known as "Quinella Louise Fitzpatrick."

The trio up in the loft suddenly noticed that the wood-framed floor-to-ceiling mirror next to the large steamer trunk was vibrating and turning lavender in color. There was always this swirling, cloud-like motion in the glass. The face once again appeared in its center. At first there was no expression and no sound — same as before, in her bathroom mirror. His eyes were closed and the face in the glass was stoic and motionless.

Far into the distant horizon, dark clouds were forming and pulsing with lightning and soft rolling thunder. The air smelled sweet, similar to when you walk into a large commercial greenhouse; it's always a pleasant and overpowering sensory experience. Gracie and Kouba Kenta left Lucinda alone so that she could visit with "Him" in private. She soon realized that she no longer looked or felt like Lucinda May Obermeyer McNichols. That was because... Quinella Louise Fitzpatrick had just arrived.

* * *

The transition was slowly taking place. Quinella felt a strange power in this transformation into a new physical shape. Remember, Lucinda was also in this body, but for now only remained as a being of electro-consciousness. She would be moving over for Quinella, for the unforeseeable future.

They would both share a life energy in Lucinda May's new body.

Gracie Aylene already knew that all of this was going to take place. Kouba Kenta Bailey was also aware of what was happening. As usual, Graham didn't have a clue.

* * *

The next revelation was the most amazing and stunning series of events that anyone could imagine. Quinella's breathing increased dramatically. Her entire body was considerably warmer and highly sensitive to touch. The transition to the new personality was taking place, including a major physical change to her body as well. Lucinda didn't know it yet, but "Quinnie" was a fifth-degree black belt and a long-distance runner, with 39 marathons to her credit so far. She was also a highly educated Rhodes Scholar. In addition to English, she was fluent in Russian, Chinese, Japanese, French, Arabic, Farsi, Hindi and Spanish.

(Maynard noticed that Lucinda May Obermeyer McNichols had just drifted off into a long sleep.)

Not surprisingly, Quinella Louise also raced motorcycles on the Grand Prix circuit. She was as fearless as she was fast. The male racers were quick to recognize Quinnie's talents as a competitor and got the heck out of her way or risked being shoved off the track with a most embarrassing big-girl nudge. She loved to whack their egos with her mesmerizing smile. She was clearly the crowd's heroine and the "darling of the track."

What became most curious and interesting was the realization that nobody knew who she was or where in the dickens she had come from. Quinnie didn't even have a mechanic or a race crew. She did have a toolbox, but no tools in it. Nope — not a screw, nut, bolt, washer or gasket in sight. Not a hacksaw or assorted wrenches, hammer, crowbar or socket set. There was, however, an empty can of WD-40. The box was a place she used to keep her sandwiches and some cosmetics, a comb and a small mirror; it was mostly girl stuff.

Quinnie would just go out and win the race, collect the trophy and wave a big "See ya later, boys," grin before disappearing until the next event, wherever that might be.

* * *

Back at the loft, the process was continuing, and certain remarkable changes kept happening to merge the forms that were in morph mode, adapting Lucinda's internal physical environment so that it would accommodate Quinella.

Feeling a bit shaky, Quinnie rose to her feet and faced the full-length mirror. Anyone would notice that she was suddenly no longer an attractive 34-year-old, as the still very lovely Lucinda was, but instead a smashingly beautiful 27-year-old, who would be known as Quinella Louise Fitzpatrick. Her hair was no longer blond but a soft and rich auburn color. She had a tan that was flawless on her wrinkle-free body. In the right light, one could detect a faint, ever so slightly brushed-up, fuzzy-wuzzy shine on the tiny hair follicles, which only enhanced the glow from her head down to her perfect toes. She also had a very cute "slight overbite."

The young skateboarder dudes in the neighborhood would surely soon refer to her as the new "hottie" at the beach and follow her everywhere they could. She couldn't help but giggle at the attention these youngsters were going to display towards her, and she would be absolutely pleased with the winks and whistles they tossed her way. She would be every bit as big a flirt as they were.

* * *

Feeling a bit dizzy, Quinella rose to her feet and suddenly noticed that her body was an amazing four inches taller. Her arms and fingers were longer, as were her legs. Her overall shape was nothing short of bikini-swimsuit "Oh boy, whackadoo" awesome. She was a living sculpture formed from the Dominic Calisto fantasy world known as "The Dreams of Dreams." She was simply beautiful. When Kouba Kenta saw her later, most of his brain sockets went *whacka ka-chunka — ka-chunk diddly-boop-pop*, with a jaw-dropping *ka-boom ka-bang*. Right away he planned to get his Rasta hair curls straightened out and to acquire a fresh, new and shinier chicken bone for the lip to celebrate this miracle.

All of a sudden, the entity referred to as "Him" opened his eyes and made direct contact with Quinella. He told her how pleased he was with the transformation. The disguise would be perfect for the "assignment." It would be a few days before this dramatic change could be fully realized, as Quinella obviously needed time to adjust. She hadn't seen herself nearly enough yet in the full-length mirror. "He," who is "Him," explained to her that the change was necessary, as the mission would be dangerous at times. It would be critical that Graham not be connected to Quinella in any way whatsoever, or the whole plan would go down in flames, literally. Secrecy had to be observed at all costs. The few men in charge of the various power groups would not hesitate to kill, on either side of the social and/or political equation.

Quinella asked "Him" whether she would be allowed to have her original Lucinda May body back when the "assignment" was over. She wondered whether Graham might want his mate back the way she used to be and look. On the other hand, he was a man, therefore part piglike, and "that there Quinnie girl" would look mighty hot to him, for sure. No need to be in a hurry here. (Maynard says this whole experience was enough to make a man eat corn on the cob backwards.)

By that evening, the transformation was complete; Lucinda did not know that she was separate now from Quinella, and vice versa. It would be so for months to come. It was set up that way for security reasons. Orientation would commence immediately. Quinnie was on a private jet within the hour, headed for Los Angeles.

A flight attendant who said his name was Dexter offered her a glass of champagne, wine, beer or anything she might want, as the Jet Star had a well-stocked bar. He also said that she could smoke or vape some really good cannabis from the Hawaiian islands should she feel like it. Quinnie declined for now, but asked if she could take it with her. She already knew how good Hawaiian Kona Gold was.

Before long the Jet Star had touched down at the smaller airport in Santa Monica. Her suite at the Four Seasons hotel was pure luxury. This would not last for long.

* * *

I need to backtrack a bit to address something important. Mentioned earlier were Graham's pets, Augie the paranoid parakeet and Spike the obese calico pussycat. It would not have been missed by most of you, my astute readers, that several years have passed by, and no way would they still be alive according to natural law. However, it would be wrong to lose these iconic characters; they can still contribute to our story. And since this extraordinary written work of art (yep, he's losing it again) is fiction, there will always be a solution. Here is how I have made it work.

Several years before, Graham's pet parakeet, Augie, had reached the point where he could hardly move at all and spent most of the daytime in his cage being depressed and barely able to chirp or feed himself. Similarly, Spike, Graham's pet pussycat, looked terrible and had lost about 30 pounds. He never meowed anymore and had a hard time coughing up fur balls. He also had given up on catching Augie; he was fresh out of paw-paw sauce, anyway. Well, it would be Gracie to the rescue. Watch for it, be patient, have a Thai stick if you can find one. Let the connoisseur in all of us blossom.

So here is the deal. Gracie took the oversized Augie from his cage and placed him on the coffee table. She then dragged a grumpy, miserable-looking Spike from under the couch and placed him next to the parakeet. She explained to them that through her magical powers their old worn-out bodies could be replaced, with their wretched conditions reversed and their bio-vessels restored into youthful beings. They would be filled with vibrant energy, health and vigor — more than they had ever experienced before. She could do this by manipulating their genomes and performing some other fancy chemical tricks regarding the resolution of nature's cosmic realignment of their DNA. It's called "reversal of chronic aging."

There was a catch — Augie and Spike would have to promise to become best of friends and treat each other with respect. No more threats against the bird, and no more screeching insults towards the cat. The two looked at each other: Augie narrowed his eyes down to slits, while Spike gave his best "Aw shucks," and said, "Let's do it," in *meow* talk, of course. This writer noticed that Spike was licking his lips when no one else was looking. We think it was a clear knee-jerk reaction. It's hard to rule out genetic programming.

Over the next few weeks, however, Augie and Spike got along very well. They watched the soap operas on television, listened to classical music and played checkers. They also pinched rocks and had fun enjoying Shark Games. Spike would give Augie rides around the house then over to the barn and loft while the perky, pumped-up bird was perched on his back. Gracie had several costumes made for them to wear. Their favorite, and mine, was when they dressed up as French Legionnaires. Augie always liked to show up as Napoléon Bonaparte. Spike preferred being Général Charles de Gaulle. They actually began to really care for each other. We know that all of you are glad to have them back in our story again. They might go on to play an incredible and decisive role in saving our planet in the very near future.

Chapter Six

Venice Beach, Chubby and the Assignment

Quinella's cottage was located on one of the typically wide walk streets in Venice, California, a couple of blocks from the beach. The main part of the 1920s residence was classic in design, with the shake shingle pitched roof and a lovers' wooden swing out on the front porch. A collection of outdoor furniture from designer Paul Mead Inc. was a perfect complement. These high-quality classic white wicker-style chairs and tables with their colourful seat cushions brought life and energy to their "living the beach life" location.

There were lots of plants and flowers attractively landscaped in behind the white picket fence that separated the cottage from the wide sidewalks. All in all, it looked very normal and charming. Inside, Quinella found some lovely period-correct furniture, including a vintage Steinway upright pedal player piano with several rolls of the classic perforated music paper.

On the main level of the house were two bedrooms, a large bathroom with a four-legged vintage bathtub and a modern kitchen. The floors were the traditional-style 10-inch-wide tongue-and-groove color-matched planks. They had been discovered at the "Omar's Fine Old Stuff" shop, in a very stylish and expensive neighborhood. "Omie," the bald and pudgy owner, was a popular Beverly Hills rare-antiques dealer and collector of precious woods. This unusual find came from the recycled lumber in his inventory of vintage honey oak stock. It was original, priceless and irreplaceable.

Quinnie loved all of it. Upstairs was a large master bedroom with Queen Anne furniture. Next to that was a snazzy loft beside the bathroom. Large bay windows to the west could be opened up, giving her a sweeping view of the Pacific Ocean, with Santa Monica and Malibu to the north. Skipping southward, one could see Marina Del Rey then Playa Del Rey, which stretches on down to the beach cities of Manhattan, Hermosa and Redondo. Beyond that were the beautiful red tile rooftops in the Malaga Cove area as one entered Palos Verdes Estates, all visible from her lovely deck. (Yes, Maynard, this writer actually lived there once, right on Via La Selva in a jungle of eucalyptus trees.)

Fancy small ceramic tubs full of daisies lined the deck. Hanging plants and flower boxes of pansies and daffodils were scattered all around. There were also a few more original pieces of the Paul Mead wicker furniture collection.

Inside, in the living room, was a hidden passageway to the basement; with the flip of a switch, the piano would swing out and expose a stairway. This opening led down to the very spooky operations room. It was electronically controlled for easy access. This very secret space was known only to the top agents at the CIA. Even the FBI wasn't aware of its existence, and nor was Interpol or MI6. The main room was outfitted with large flat-screen TVs, huge computer data storage units, tables, chairs and other machines that one would expect to find at NASA or in a covert military workplace.

Interestingly enough, there was also a duplicate of the floor-to-ceiling mahogany-framed mirror, same as the one in the loft at the McNichols' Rushtuk farm back in Idaho. Well, there obviously had to be a place for "Him" to show up, right? It was the secure connection to Quinella Louise Fitzpatrick. (Maynard says, "Stay with me on this, folks — it gets much better.")

The following morning, Quinnie was to begin her orientation in downtown Los Angeles at Chubby's Soup and Burger Emporium. This would be the first of her many meetings and adventures with Chubby — who, by the way, was a key figure in the CIA's plan to save the free world. Chub's real name was O'Gooha Bhah Tootoe, which in Zulu means "Fat Little Bugger." How charming.

"The Emporium" was housed in a really cool old shack built in 1950 or so. County records were hard to come by, as it had changed ownership so many times. The shape of the building was post-WW II in design, with a red brick front and a shake-style cedar roof. The entrance featured a heavy Dutch door with large framed-in windows and flower boxes on each side. Out on the patio were tables and chairs with colorful umbrellas, all sitting on real fescue grass. A thick eight-foot-tall bougainvillea hedge loaded with bright orange, white, pink and velvety red flowers surrounded the area for privacy and comfort.

Inside there were huge old leather-covered booths with a circular step up, located around the perimeter of the lounge. Out on the floor were separate round tables and wooden high-back chairs. The new owners had randomly filled in the center of the lower section behind the barstools with odd pieces of furniture.

The bar itself was still original and perfect. Its massive design was the dominant feature of the interior; the overall length was 18 to 20 feet, the wrap-around curve down at the end adding another four to five feet in length to its unique "J" shape. The bar-top's surface had a smooth, rolled out and raised edge that pushed outward towards the patrons. The wood was hand-ground, sanded, and grooved from burled walnut, which would be impossible to find today. As an antique, it was considered priceless.

The swivel-mounted metal bar seats and stools were custom-fitted with harvested and refurbished pieces and parts from local salvage yards specializing in vintage farm tractors. The tractor seats had been repainted flat black to match the rest of the rustic decor. They were very distinctive, great-looking and comfortable. If you have ever been on a farm in Nebraska, then you know what they look like. If you haven't, well then you don't. You are just going to have to search this out yourself. It's worth it. Participate — I can't be expected to do everything.

Mounted across from the back bar, starting at the same height as the bar surface, was a gigantic saltwater aquarium that some said took thousands of gallons to fill. The slightly inward-curved tank was eleven feet tall, and five feet across from the inside face to the back side. A mural had been painted spanning the full length of the tank's inside back wall. The electronically controlled artwork displayed a detailed and accurate image of a naturally dramatic interior similar to the Carlsbad Caverns in southern New Mexico: lots of stalactites and stalagmites, scattered throughout with mini-waterfalls cascading in steps and spilling into clear pools.

All of this was computer-generated. It was done in such a way that one believed that the cavern was actually real and very deep, complete with sound effects sweeping towards the rear and into the darkness. The lighting inside the tank's cavern could be turned up or down depending on the mood of the patrons or the bartender, who was usually Chubby. The fish seemed to go in and out at will. When looking at it lengthwise from across the room, one saw that it stretched to nearly 20 feet long, which was almost the full length of the bar.

The tank was chock full of very colorful exotic fish, including zebras, guppies, clownfish, dottyfish, blennies and masked bannerfish. There were two small mako sharks, a few sea turtles and a manta ray. Finally, a couple of scary-looking eels and one shy octopus named Lucille. Most of the regulars just called her Lucy.

There were many more interesting things to look at, including plants of all kinds. Inside the tank, near the curve, was an aging vessel tipped upward; it was the starboard side of what was left of the sunken front quarter of a very old small wooden sailing ship. Some said it had been used to transport slaves — possibly tiny slaves; perhaps they were from Pygmy tribes. Chubby knew the truth but wasn't saying.

There were also several of the obligatory old pirate treasure chests strewn about with their lids open. Gold and silver coin had been spilled out on the sand, next to the porcelain and gold Fabergé vases.

All the booty was strung out along the sculpted white sand floor of the tank, including long strands of pearls still strung together and other rare jewelry pieces.

Synchronized colored lights pulsed and danced around inside the aquarium when the music was playing. Every time an Elvis tune was selected, the mako sharks raced each other from one end of the tank past the curved section in the middle, then over to the end and back. Some of the patrons decided to set up regular sports gambling to bet on which shark would win the race. Since the two sharks were identical, there were always arguments over just whose shark finished first. Well, fist fights, beer-mug tossing and stool throwing over the disagreements got out of hand. So Chubby had to shut down "the track" whenever Elvis was playing. Lucy the octopus had a "screw this silly nonsense" attitude and simply went into hiding. All the other fish just scattered and tried not to get run over.

Submerged in the middle of the tank was a vintage 1940 Harley-Davidson motorcycle. It appeared as if it had plunged off a cliff and directly into the tank. The bike was still upright at about a 45-degree angle, pointed downward nose first. The front wheel was buried about halfway into the sand. Facing the patrons sitting at the bar and perched on the Harley with his bony fingers still clinging to the handlebars was a full-size human skeleton. Somebody had named him Garth McTavish. He was wearing his full biker gang leather jacket and riding pants, along with the classic black engineer side-buckle stomper boots, complete with silver shoulder chains that wound through the epaulets of his "Full Patch" jacket and his motorcycle cap. Noticeable was the tiny braided gold rope above its visor, signifying his rider's rank. Garth had been a high-level officer, it seemed. (Maynard wasn't sure exactly where or when.)

Garth was poised in an aggressive Marlon Brando–style racing position. (Maynard says that if you remember the hit movie *The Wild One* then you are older than he is.) By the way, you can check it out; the flick is on Netflix and YouTube.

Many of the patrons and other bums would agree that the reason for Garth still being there in the tank was his devotion and commitment to the Harley-Davidson motorcycle company. (Maynard thinks that is entirely possible.)

There was another antique that was also a prime object at Chubby's Soup and Burger Emporium.

Against the far wall was a restored antique stand-alone Wurlitzer jukebox complete with working neon lighting encapsulated in large glass tubes between the shaped chrome channels on the sides and then curving across the top of the unit. This classic player still worked and featured the real oldies. The artists on the selector included Slim Whitman, Willie Nelson, Elvis Presley, Bing Crosby, The Andrews Sisters, Burl Ives, Perry Como, Patti Page, Vic Damone, Tommy Dorsey, Glen Miller, Stan Kenton, Liberace and many more. The original "78" records were very fragile; they could get scratched and break easily.

Chubby had made sure that the Lawrence Welk records were thrown out. Myron Floren and Larry Hooper supposedly sent letters of protest, but they were told that Myron's accordion would be tossed into the tank along with Larry's piano if either of them showed up. A poster of Uncle Sam pointing his finger at you near the restroom said: "Beware!! Play the Accordion — Go to Jail!"

Hidden beneath the old jukebox was a stairway that led down to the control room stuck deep in an underground dungeon — a space outfitted very much like the secret basement in Quinella's beach house. It was an electronic masterpiece with all the same computers, gadgets and techno stuff as her cottage in Venice. There was also another full-length mirror for the swirling-lavender-cloud moments when "He" showed up as "Him."

The ambiance in Chubby's very quaint pub was pleasant and friendly. Quinnie would add her personal touch and make it even better. The breakfast and lunch business was huge and barely manageable. Happy hour was the usual drinks and munchies only. Chubby always closed the place up by nine on weekdays and by ten on Fridays. He had decided to not be open on Saturdays and Sundays, much to the chagrin of our local spaced-out fish tank addicts and other stoners.

Our hero, "Mr. C," was a Zulu from Zambia; they are the largest members of all the African tribes and also, by the way, among the tallest people on Earth. "The Chubster" was 8 feet 7 inches tall and tipped the scales at a little over 425, give or take a couple of pounds. Who was gonna ask? He also had a shiny gold incisor tooth, and when he smiled you could see it from about a mile away — or at least it seemed as if you could. His silver-sprinkled black hair was styled up into a two-inch-tall mini-Afro do. He also had a pair of snazzy emerald and ruby earrings that jingled and jangled around his charming, youthful face.

Chubby could control the moment anywhere, anytime, with his deep-set and piercing blue eyes; they came in handy when he needed to be forceful with rowdy drunks raising hell in the bar. If you didn't pay attention when he wanted you to behave or something like that, he would just growl — then you did it, and right now, not later. Someone said he was so strong that he could "futz up" a machine shop's full-size iron anvil with his bare hands.

Smart? Well, you can check this out. Chubby just happened to have a doctorate from the University of South Africa, qualifying him as an expert at collating, identifying and comparing various international social mores and cultural behaviours. The info was all logged in the current United States database of the world's history near Washington, DC. This included any and all computer systems. He had a huge compilation of information on our so-called modern nations. Two years before, he had received a Fulbright Scholarship and then a Senior Honours degree from Oxford in the United Kingdom. He was also one really bad dude when he needed to be. Did I mention that he also had a photographic memory? This was going to come in handy when Quinnie got going on her task of saving the remaining civilized world.

Strong as Quinella was, she would also need plenty of assistance from Gracie Aylene and Kouba Kenta Bailey. Don't forget, Uncle KK was a munitions and explosives wizard thanks to the US Military. Chicken bone or no chicken bone. He could blow up almost anything he wanted to.

* * *

As she began her training under the steady guidance of Chubby, Quinella set out to learn what she could about the world's nine power groups, which essentially controlled all the forces that had governed modern civilizations over the previous two centuries:

1. **Hasta Luego Cuanto La Gusta: blind control of the western hemisphere**
2. **CIA, FBI and US and Canadian military forces**
3. **Mexican and South American Pinto and Coffee Bean Coalition**
4. **Interpol–Britain–Scandinavia–MI6 and European Congress**

5. **Russian Mafia, KGB and Baltic Nations Consortium**
6. **Middle Eastern Turkish-Syrian-Iraqi and Iranian Desert Republics**
7. **China, India, Pakistan, Indonesia, Himalayan and Yeti Plebeians**
8. **Israel and Golan Heights Gefilte Pescado Grenadiers**
9. **Casa Bailarín los Bandidos de la Sombra ("The Shadow Dancers")**

One of her first tasks was to learn to recognize each group's individual personality, strengths and weaknesses. Quinnie studied the world powers via some super-slick computer-hacking tricks and logged the info into her mind, gathering all of their history and their relative importance. The goal, of course, was to eliminate any evil elements aiming to thwart the principles of democracy valued by the free world and to eventually return the organizations to a place of respect and dignity. That is, all except number 9; the Bailarín twins had to be stopped and crushed, as they were wicked to the core.

Casa Bailarín sought to annihilate the other eight control groups by getting them to war against each other. They wanted to destroy the status quo, then rebuild and re-form the globe's remaining populations. These would be divided into workers, pawns and technical breeders. All remaining people would be tested and placed into their genetically programmed and environmentally determined social pods, as long as they were functioning within the agenda. Those poor souls who didn't fit the mold would be vaporized immediately — *Allez Poof.*

Quinella was excited to learn about the power players, and she was a whiz when it came to plowing through all the background information on them. Her plan was to address, access, then infiltrate. The unsavory elements in the first eight of these groups were in the process of going down in flames and would be destroyed fairly easily, as they were busy taking each other out. It was the ninth and most hidden bunch of thugs that she would struggle with. Very little was known about them, and many argued that they were simply fiction. It would turn out that they not only did exist but were the most powerful and vicious of all the world's control organizations. They were also the oldest and could trace their roots back at least 700 years. The Casa Bailarín los Bandidos de la Sombra members referred to themselves as "The Shadow Dancers," a somewhat rough translation of the Spanish name.

"The Dancers" were the most secretive — virtually invisible — and no one knew how the group operated or just who belonged. It was unclear how many members there might be, how they were selected for membership, or if it was a cross-section of like-minded criminals from many countries.

Quinnie learned that they were the most sinister and deadly when they felt that the elimination of some presumed foe was necessary. The executions of those chosen for disposal were swift, silent, untraceable and all conducted under a cloak of secrecy by an inner group known as Muerte y Besa Mi Tush, Por Favor.

The Shadow Dancers were the real power behind the IMF, who everyone thought was in control of the major world banks. Ha, they were merely administrators and bookkeepers. The "Dancers" monitored the world's inventory of precious metals, such as steel, aluminum, uranium, lead, copper, molybdenum, gold and silver, and related categories. Concrete, rubber and all plastics were watched full-time for quality and shortages. And, of course, the cartel was busy supposedly protecting all the fresh water in our lakes and streams.

They also took on the enormous task of overseeing what was being dumped into the oceans. An educated group of specialists worked diligently on problems relating to the growing scourge of pollution, especially plastics. Raw sewage and other petroleum products were always a serious concern, as well. Additional efforts were undertaken to oversee oil, lumber and all food production and to ensure that animal populations were healthy. One of the most scrutinized sectors was the pharmaceutical industry, as those companies couldn't be trusted for honesty.

The Casa Bailarín los Bandidos de la Sombra were already set in motion to be in full control of the world's military. Finally, it was observed that close management of the transportation industry, including bus, truck, auto and airline companies, was now a reality. However, the "Dancers" didn't pay much attention to the clothing industry and the manufacturing cartels; they knew that some guy named "Ralph" would be in charge of that, anyway. It was assumed that the creation of the embroidered logo of that silly pony with a rider swinging a golf club or something was what had given him all the necessary credibility. He was therefore more or less left alone. After all, the dude is a billionaire, for crying out loud. In any case, the shirts and neckties are nice.

Ralph would remain untouched for now. It was nonetheless rumored that he might be challenged in the future by a brilliant new designer. (Maynard heard that Giorgio Versace Armani was recently seen walking over to a company called "Embroideries R Us" in New York City, carrying a croquet mallet and a boxing glove... hmmm.)

All communications within Casa Bailarín los Bandidos de la Sombra were secretly encrypted, with access being limited to the top scrutineers of classified information. They would be received by and given to only the highest level of the most trusted membership for decoding. Quinella and Chubby were amazed to find out later that the entire organization was run, at the best of times, by nine lieutenant generals. The total number of members in The Shadow Dancers remained unknown.

Chapter Seven

A Cyanide Evening in Carmel

After several days of Quinella's training, Chubby was on the phone very early to her secret cell line on a muggy-smoggy Los Angeles summer morning. It wasn't hot, just bad air quality, and you could smell it. Rain was in the forecast for the evening; that would surely be a welcome relief.

They were already pretty good friends and Quinnie said, "What's up, Chub ol' pal?" His voice was cold and not full of his usual powerful, high and ready-to-party voice rhythms and vibrations. Later she told him that he sounded like somebody who was just about to croak. Well, it was even worse. Turned out that Laboratory #23, the most hidden and protected facility at the Livermore Nuclear Labs in California, had been broken into during the night. At least 40 to 50 soldiers, special police and other high-level operatives had been found unconscious but alive.

Not a single security alarm had sounded throughout the invasion. There was no sign of any violence; in fact the victims were casual about the whole thing as they regained their sensibilities. Nothing was missing and no one had a valid explanation as to just what had happened or why. They were, to a person, relaxed and unconcerned, as if nothing had happened. One of the soldiers wanted to know if breakfast was going to be served, or should he go out? It would be a while before the pieces of this puzzle started to come together.

Quinella raced in record time along the Santa Monica freeway towards downtown Los Angeles to Chubby's Soup and Burger Emporium. She was driving her recently acquired dark blue 1972 Alfa Romeo Veloce. She liked the older roadsters better than the newer high-tech computer-driven models. To her, all the romance was lost in the button-less knob-less, almost self-driving sports cars. She would rather drive this puppy herself.

Where was the fun in just sitting behind the wheel, knowing that some Silicon Valley nanotech dude was going to guide her to a destination via an electronic bucketful of satellite wizardry? What would some bowtie-wearing nerd know about observing the white markings on black gauges and the magic sounds made by the multiple clicks of dash-mounted toggle switches?

Quinnie was a "slide your foot on that left-side pedal and let's double-clutch those gears up and down" kinda gal. She figured, "With my other foot on the gas, I'm ready to twist that tachometer needle up over 7000 RPMs and wrench out 500-plus steaming, screaming Italian horsepower." How she never got stopped by the traffic cops or photo radar was a mystery. She wanted to go to work on her racing motorcycle at least some of the time. Chubby said no, and he said it with his "Don't even think about arguing with me" look. She just said to herself, *I'll ride on the weekends.*

Ha! Guess what, "Toots" — you don't get weekends off when you're busy saving the world from a vicious gang of cutthroats bent on total control of their designer-engineered population regions.

Quinnie arrived at the EMP (abbreviation for the Emporium) in record time, then climbed up onto one of the recycled tractor seats at the bar. She reached across and gave Chubby a big smooch on his cheek. "Let's get to work and stop these sorry no-good rats." The Chubster was a little startled but also grateful that Quinella was on the side of right. He appreciated her energy.

It was the government officials who finally determined that some kind of knockout punch with a chemical vapor had been used to send all those men and women in Livermore into nighty-night mode. Well, they weren't really sure, but it was critical to report at least something to their superiors even if it wasn't accurate. The authorities were not even close, as we shall see.

Chubby brought Quinella up to speed with all the information he had for now. He said it would be a good idea if they went up to Lab #23 in Livermore that weekend to check it out. They both had the necessary security clearances to go just about anywhere they wanted.

Quinnie said, "Great, let's do it — the Alfa is already gassed up and I'll make us a picnic lunch that can't be beat." Chubby was moving back into the kitchen, laughing his large rear end off, when Quinnie, looking very puzzled, asked, "What...?" With a wink and a grin, our large Zulu guy looked Miss

Motorcycle Pants in the eye and said, "Did you want me to ride in your car, or should I wear it? Do you not see how large I am?"

Well, Quinnie took a minute and ascertained that he was in fact quite correct. She blinked and, in the middle of an award-wining natural face blush, thought quietly to herself, *Yep, I'll bet he's very "large" indeed.* Quinella then suggested that perhaps they should drive up in Chubby's special-edition military version of the Ford Motor Company's all-terrain vehicle known as the Raptor. Chub was already onto that. Duh?

Saturday morning rolled around and our heroes were on their way early to beat the LA traffic. Chubby had decided to drive up to Santa Barbara on California Interstate 101, then eventually move over and join with Highway 1 on the coast, heading due north towards San Luis Obispo. They would cut across to have lunch near Morro Bay.

It was a beautiful day, with clear blue skies and a gentle onshore breeze. Quinella had made a world-class picnic lunch for them: homemade garlic pumpernickel bread, sliced barbecue pork shoulder, aged cheddar with minced jalapeno peppers, spicy mustard and avocado mayo. She also had made some delicious strawberry gummy bears for desert. Always an excellent travel treat. Right, Jasper? (Maynard says we should check with Kouba Kenta Bailey.)

Well, the lunch and the gummy bears did help with being able to grin at the ocean and those silly seagulls, who never had a solid plan about anything they ever did. Quinnie had also made sun tea on Friday. They didn't talk much, and she sensed that the big boy had a lot on his mind. She was right; he had new information that he would have to share with her very soon, since she was his partner and needed to know as much as him.

Chubby thanked her for the fabulous lunch and helped pack up — they still had a long day ahead of them. The pair decided to stick to their decision to wind their way up the coast on Highway 1 through Big Sur. They would pass through the Esalen Institute Retreat (a place where some are sure they specialize in "mind adjustment.") Yep, then it was on to Carmel for the night. This magnificent route is one of our nation's most famous scenic drives.

The area's environment is one of unparalleled beauty, filled with powerful visual and auditory drama from the pounding of the Pacific Ocean against the lush, grass-covered bluffs. Many say it is as lovely as the west coast of Scotland. Some say not. (Maynard says, pick one.)

The Ford Raptor was a handful on the seemingly endless series of sharp curves. However, given its sheer size and power, it was nevertheless very comfortable. The independent suspension and 4 x 4 torsional drive is amazingly quiet while cruising. The motor has a sweet, purring sound unless you stomp your foot down on the accelerator hard. It responds instantly with the roar of a Saturn rocket as the twin turbos kick in and awaken the nearly 800 supercharged horsepower of the V-8 engine. It's no sissy. It was definitely "giddy up" and go. Quinella couldn't wait to drive it. She would no doubt be called on to be the "pilot in charge" many times.

The fearsome twosome rolled into Carmel just before sunset. Chubby had booked two suites at the Pine Inn on Ocean Avenue. It was built around 1889 and was originally known as the Hotel Carmelo. It still had its classic charm. The hotel was in the middle of downtown and a few short blocks to the beach near the famous cypress tree that gets photographed far too often.

Quinnie's suite was the Queen Isabella Boudoir and was stunning, with beautiful furniture, classic textured floral wallpaper, a wood-burning fireplace and a private balcony facing the ocean. Chub's room was called the Viceroy and had a self-serve bar that was stocked with two kinds of Scotch whisky, aged Irish bourbon, Russian vodka and very expensive Italian red and French white wines. The sitting parlor offered a lovely ocean view. For Chubby's comfort, he had the "manly" double king-size vibrating massage bed and a lot of oversized hand-carved wooden furniture, mostly pine and some walnut. All of this was good when you consider that this man is eight feet seven inches tall. Right away you got a sense that he had stayed there before. *Correcto-mundo, mi Capitán.*

The restaurant was near the lobby and was situated inside a large arboretum. It was outfitted with glass-topped tables and matching white metal chairs with beautiful floral patterns pressed into them. There were mature tropical plants all around, creating a cozy and perfect jungle-like atmosphere. You could almost feel and hear Tarzan swinging through on one of his always convenient rope vines. In the background he would be looking for Jane or possibly Cheetah, their pet chimpanzee. "Boy" (their son) had grown up and was a dancing cross-dresser at San Francisco's Pavilion. Ah-Lee-Ahl... Lee-Ally-Ally-Ahl... Lee-Ahl-Lee-Ally-Ally-Ahl. I don't know what happened — probably the gummy bears. (Maynard has already apologized, but he applauds those of you who recognized Tarzan's yell.)

After a short walk on the beach, they returned to the hotel for a shower, then a sandy-sponge body-skin scrape for Quinnie, with a sweet Sativa cannabis nugget and a big-girl toke on the vape. Chubby had a hot soak in the king-size marble tub. They agreed to meet in the restaurant for dinner at eight. Chubby put on his dark blue blazer jacket, a white broadcloth cotton dress shirt with a wildly jazzed-up paisley print silk ascot and British tan corduroy jeans. For comfort and style, he was out of his fatigues and the military boots. He chose his calfskin leather penny loafers. A post-preppy fashion statement, for sure.

Quinella, who was trying her best not to giggle too much from the effects of the "weed," wore her perfectly tailored soft-twill-weave jumpsuit in black from the celebrated designer Micheal Kors, made out of brushed Moroccan merino wool. As an accent, she chose small pieces of Southwestern turquoise and silver jewelry. The look was very simple but elegant — one ring, one bracelet, one necklace. As she walked, her long, perfectly fluffed-up auburn hair bounced around her lovely tanned shoulders, framing her beautiful angelic face and those knuckle-deep dimples passed on from Lucinda... Double-freaking WOW!!!

Chubby selected a table near the tall, spiraled fountain, which spilled water into a pool decorated with large floating lily pads, giving the common goldfish a shaded sanctuary. The orange koi from Japan and the white speckle fish would look at the spare change tossed in the pool, supposedly for good luck (whose luck?) by the idiots and the sometimes drunk crowd. One might think that if the fish could talk, they would probably say something like, "What in the heck are we supposed to do with all these coins and other junk that gets tossed in here? How would you like it if a regiment of jellyfish and an army of turtles fouled your hot tub? Hey, how about you tossing or flipping in a nice juicy worm or moth, or how about finger-flicking us a slow-moving tasty bug in here, you drunk bozo slob. No more coin, okay?" (Maynard agreed that goldfish had a right to their opinions.)

Chubby was speechless upon seeing Quinella, but the big Zulu guy got a grip and was glad that he had already ordered the wine; he was almost ready to speak but didn't want to sound like a canary that had just been stepped on.

The wine was a very expensive French Bordeaux called "Cyrano de Schnozzola," vintage 1938. Quinnie appreciated his choice, as it was rich, full-bodied and properly decanted. The waiter brought the menus, which were conservative in scope but offered more than enough to appeal to the fine-dining crowd. They chose to go for the gourmet buffet instead. It was loaded with all the really good appetizer stuff. Chubby decided that this evening would be about chit-chat stories, jokes, tall tales and the enjoyment of each other's company. The business of saving the world could wait until morning.

The evening moved on and became dreamlike for both of them. I'm pretty sure that the second bottle of "Schnozzola," along with the vapes of Humboldt County's finest cannabis and the exquisite dinner enhanced the mood. Ya think? Love those government expense accounts. Yippie Ki-Yay, Ki-Yo.

Well, as wonderful as the meal was, it was time to adjourn for the night. They were waiting for their waiter, whom Quinnie had nicknamed "Packy the Pickle," to bring the bill.

All of a sudden Quinella sensed that they were being watched. She had had an inkling earlier but dismissed it, as the vibe wasn't that strong. Quinnie mentioned it to Chubby, and he had picked up on it as well. The only thing a little askew that they had both observed, was that the two well-dressed gentlemen sitting across the dining room were identical twins, probably in their early forties. They were wearing dark suits, white shirts and plain neckties. The men were nearly out of sight behind the water fountain. It just didn't look quite right, and Chubby and Quinnie also realized that they had been there all evening.

Quinella had noticed that the right hand of one of the men was tattooed black from the wrist down. Chubby explained to her that the black hand signified the status of ultimate rank and power in the criminal world, exceeding even that of a Sicilian godfather.

The "Twins" soon departed, leaving a black business card on their table which represented a sinister and planned direct purpose. The Shadow Dancers' "coat of arms" signature was printed on the front, and their names on the back: Beto and Chaco Bailarín. The raised lettering was done in red, and their phone number was within the Los Angeles area code system.

"The Shadow Dancers":
Beto and Chaco Bailarín

"Packy" returned with the bill and looked very nervous. His hands were trembling. Chubby suddenly realized that he didn't have his weapon on him. Guess what, folks — Quinella Louise Fitzpatrick had her 9 mm Beretta in her nifty little black clutch purse with all the shiny silver sequins on it. You can be sure it was loaded. ("You betchum, Red Ryder.")

Chubby signed the bill to his account after adding a huge tip and handed it back to Packy but didn't let go. With his piercing blue eyes and massive size, the Chubster said, using his usual persuasion, "You *WILL* meet us in my suite in five minutes. Don't be late, or I will have to come and find you. I can assure you, it would not be a good idea." Packy the Pickle just gulped and set a new record for blurting out the fastest "YES, SIR" of his life.

Back in Chubby's suite and waiting for Packy to arrive, Quinella asked if it would be okay if she poured herself a stiff drink. Chub said okay and would she be kind enough to fix one for him as well, please. Two double Scotch and waters were coming right up. Quinnie was knocking her drink back like a redneck hanging off a barstool, when Chubby raced across the room yelling for her not to drink it. He slapped the glass from her hand. Too late — she had already swallowed half of it. The big guy had sniffed his glass just a few seconds before and detected an odor he was familiar with.

Yep, the Scotch had been tampered with, alright. We got ourselves some high-octane deadly cyanide poison here, folks. Quinnie dropped to the floor like a hard sack of Irish potatoes, her body shaking violently from head to toe. Deep purple mucky goo was foaming and starting to ooze slowly out the side of her mouth. Her skin had a greenish sheen to it. Chubby raced out of the room, heading for the lobby to seek help. As he rounded the corner, our unlucky "Pickle-Pluckin' Packy," the waiter, was flattened out like a banana pancake. Poor ol' Pack didn't see the Chubster version of the freight train coming. *Ka-Pow!! Ka-Squoosh!!* and *Ka-Smush!!* (Maynard says that's for our *Batman* fans.)

Finally at the reception desk, Chubby grabbed the night clerk and said, "Call an ambulance now and see if there is a doctor registered at the hotel." With that, our Big Guy rushed back to attend to Quinnie and noticed that Packy wasn't on the floor in the hallway where he had been squashed flat by what could be described as a determined "killer tackle" straight from someone who could have played for the Detroit Lions in their mighty backfield.

Into the room charged a very anxious giant Zulu only to be shocked to discover that Quinella was nowhere in sight, nor was Packy. The plot had therefore thickened... as the old saying goes.

The medics arrived, finding no one to assist, followed by eight or nine local police. The ranking officer said, "Let's get some facts here, folks." (Maynard says, "Just the facts, ma'am... just the facts.") "We need to make sense of this event and to have a plan." Chubby grabbed two skinny cops and screamed a tribal war chant into their ears, bursting their perfectly good eardrums. Then, with a hands-on upper-body power move, he bashed their heads together and asked, "Is this making any sense yet?"

Well, a swarm of blue-suited cops finally took Chubby to the floor and handcuffed him. It was about to get a lot stranger. The two cops with the busted eardrums would be known from then on as Huh? and Uh-huh?

On the way over to the county jail in Monterey, Chubby made up some story that was almost believable, and the police chief was sympathetic. However, a problem arose when the hotel registry was checked and there was no one on the books listed as Quinella Louise Fitzpatrick.

The suspicious Twins had disappeared. Quinnie's suite was thoroughly checked and the cops found nothing that belonged to her. The Raptor was also missing from the parking garage. The attendants swore they had never seen the four-wheel-drive beast.

The next day, all the employees were questioned, but this didn't reveal much. The Twins weren't on the registry, either, but they occasionally were seen at the inn for lunch, sometimes with another man, who would become a big part of this drama later on. They had also been noticed about town in other stores. Well-dressed twins aren't hard to spot. Observers all agreed that they were of Spanish decent, possibly from Mexico or perhaps Brazil.

Following two nights in the Monterey jail, Chubby was released after a secret high-level phone call came in from Washington, DC. The Monterey Chief of Police said nothing to anyone, and all charges against Chub were dropped. One of the officers with a busted eardrum was heard saying, "WHAT?" and "UH-HUH?" The other one responded with "HUH? — excuse me?"

Chubby didn't know what to do. Should he go on to Livermore, or back to Los Angeles? The Raptor had been found in a ditch but not damaged. He did have the good sense to call ahead and have a sign put up at the Soup and Burger Emporium saying "CLOSED FOR REMODELING." It was highly suspicious, as there were no workers, only a redheaded caretaker named Merle who would show up to feed the fish and water the grass out on the patio. He would also spend hours in the secret downstairs dungeon where he wasn't allowed, doing who knows what. The situation at hand made you want to do the "Who's on First Joke." (For those of you who don't know the joke, it was an incredibly funny skit done by two very famous comedians named Abbot and Costello.) I highly recommend a Google-up, or you will never know who's on first, what's on second and I don't know who's on third. It ain't Merle. (Maynard is going nuts right about now.)

Chubby's cellphone buzzed and a muffled voice with a Spanish accent said, "If you want to see Quinella again, you will do exactly as you are told." He heard Quinnie's voice in the background say, "Please help me!!" Chub wasn't sure she was still alive. Was it a recording, or was it her? He wanted more proof, but he also knew that would be dangerous. Our Chubber decided to skip Livermore for now and return to LA. He blasted his way over to Interstate 5 and roared the Raptor towards southern California. He was able to get police clearance all the way. The drab olive-colored, overpowered beast chewed up the distance in record time. Now all he could do was wait. Hard for him to do, as O'Gooha Bhah Tootoe was not a patient man.

At 3 a.m., his secret phone rang. Chubby was awake instantly. He had already assumed that The Shadow Dancers had their mitts on Quinella, and the few who knew about them were aware of the ruthlessness with which they could and would operate. A Spanish-accented voice said, "If you do as we say, we will spare her and see that she is safely returned. As of now, she is unharmed; if you fail, we will send her back in pieces, starting with her feet." A cold chill went over our brave giant. He believed they would do it. Chubby therefore agreed to anything they wanted.

First he wanted proof that she was in fact okay right at that moment, then he said, "If so, I will proceed with your requests." Quinella was put on the phone and in a calm voice said, "I'm okay — do what you think is right."

The Dancer's voice was later found out to belong to Beto Bailarín. He was the thinker and planner and clearly the stronger of the Twins. Chaco carried out all the dirty work. He was vicious and enjoyed seeing many people suffer.

The first request was for Chubby to send all the information he had on the eight other power groups in his data systems. A special code was developed so that Chub could send the encrypted info to Casa Bailarín's own spy satellite. He was to do this in 24 hours, or Quinnie's left foot would be hacksawed off just above the ankle and sent over via registered mail to the EMP. The best Chubby could possibly do was to send bulk documents to the satellite and hope for the best. He did know that most of the other eight power groups were in trouble and couldn't last much longer, anyway.

This was all taking a terrible toll on the Chubster. It was because he had become aware as they were having their dinner in the Pine Inn's arboretum that he was going to be very much in love with Quinella Louise Fitzpatrick. He didn't want to be, but it had happened anyway. Now he had to rescue her somehow at all costs. He wondered how much more The Shadow Dancers would want. If the info he gave them could help destroy the other eight power groups, then he wouldn't have to deal with that task. Our Chubber didn't care, as long as he could get her back safely and of course all in one piece.

Chapter Eight

A Zulu Interrogation: O'Gooha Bhah Tootoe

Well, back at the farm over in Rushtuk, Idaho, Gracie Aylene McNichols and Kouba Kenta Bailey were wondering about a lot of things. Mostly, they were concerned over the safety of Lucinda, who for now was still neatly tucked into what had become Quinnie's body. A few days before, loud snoring had been heard coming from near the tall wood-framed magic mirror in the loft out in the barn. Gracie was checking it every day to see if "He," who is known as "Him," had left any messages for her. She worried about her mom, and there was no communication from Quinella, the morphee.

Did they speak to one another? Could they sense that both were living together in Lucinda May Obermeyer McNichols' updated and reworked body?

Gracie needed to find out what was happening. She went to the mirror often to request a visit with "Him." She had the power to get all this information herself, but out of respect she would go through the channels and comply with tradition in seeking wishes and wisdom from "Him." It was a good choice. Gracie wanted more information on O'Gooha Bhah Tootoe — who, as we all know, was our giant Zulu, affectionately known as Chubby, the Chub or the Chubster. He was the government-funded owner of Chubby's Soup and Burger Emporium in Los Angeles, California.

Gracie kept her father happy by pretending to be Lucinda on the phone. She could disguise her voice to sound exactly like her mom's, and Graham bought it. Our sweet little special Gracie Aylene would blush when Graham talked about his and Lucinda's relationship and how much he missed her. He often spoke about the intimate details the two of them had shared over the years. Sometimes there was a little too much information. Ya think? However, she was glad that her parents were both romantic and still such hot lovers. They seriously wanted each other all the time, and they for sure wanted to continue their steamy romance, even after 20-plus years.

Graham was swamped with work — always fighting for and getting the benefits that would go directly to the citizens of Idaho. He was also called upon to serve on many national committees, as well as a few scary international programs. He was learning a lot and was well respected by his peers in the United States Senate.

Soon Gracie was able to make contact with "Him" and was advised to go to Los Angeles and meet with Chubby. She wasn't quite sure how to explain why Lucinda and Quinnie were both in the new version of the same single body. She would just have to convince the Chubster by using a few of her powerful gifts. Kouba Kenta Bailey would, as always, be her backup and mentor. Gracie thought that it was time for a big show, as the clock was ticking. She would need to be on her "A game" and very creative, for she knew that Chubby was no fool. Sincerity and a flawless sense of timing were essential; it would have to be an "eye popper" of an event.

It took two days to drive to Los Angeles in Kouba Kenta's 1958 Volkswagen Microbus and find this Zulu prince of a man, who was working his magic at the EMP. Gracie had a plan and had been given directions on how to find Chubby's soup and burger joint. She had requested and received complete pictures of the bar, the cozy lounge, the Wurlitzer, the swiveling antique tractor seats, the surrounding fixtures and, of course, the enormous aquarium.

Gracie and Kouba found and entered the establishment at about 11 a.m., just before the lunch crowd started filing in. They introduced themselves to Chubby and explained why they were there. It was a visual skit, for sure, especially when one took a hard look at Kouba Kenta Bailey, an albino with soft pink eyes and an unruly all-white Rasta-styled hairdo with four or five two-foot-long dreadlocks hanging off his shoulders. Then ponder the unlikelihood of a gorgeous 17-year-old girl with a glow that couldn't be fathomed while she turned her shimmer wick up and down. She had to be sure that Chubby accepted and trusted them and knew they were there to help rescue both Quinnie and Lucinda.

For a final convincer, Gracie instructed Kouba to strip down to his leopardskin bikini skivvies and submerge himself in the aquarium. She told him to sit quietly on the sand next to Garth, who was still in the tank riding on the Harley. Just then, as if a whistle had blown, the tropical fish, the sharks and the sea turtles all positioned themselves in an organized military formation and swam several laps around inside the tank. They were being led by Orville, the manta ray, and Lucille, the shy octopus, who was riding on "Orvie"'s wing. Suddenly, as if on a cue from Gracie, Kouba Kenta disappeared backwards into the watery cavern — or it seemed that way — only to return moments later wearing an exact duplicate of Elvis Presley's heavy gold-framed sunglasses and his silver-sparkle Las Vegas costume with the long bright red sash around the waist. He was holding an old classical guitar and looking as if he was a "rootin'-tootin'-shootin" crazy albino badass Rasta gunslinger. ("Don't be cruel, ooh-ooh-ooh..., to a heart that's true, ooh-ooh-ooh.")

The Wurlitzer lit up all on its own, and cranked out Elvis Presley's "Don't Be Cruel" hit song from the late fifties. Kouba's dreadlocks swung back and forth while his hips swung forth and back. The sharks went crazy and raced themselves to exhaustion. Kouba Kenta then sat down quietly in the tank, on the sand, next to Garth, for the next two hours with no noticeable movement or any obvious or natural way of being able to breathe while sitting underwater. He didn't need any, as the universe was at work with him through Gracie and her magical powers. It was a special "one-sided ear wiggle plus four eye blinks followed by a hitchhiker's thumb-and-forefinger snapping" moment. Some would later say that it was because "He" had shown up as "Him." (Maynard says, "And there you have it, sports fans.")

Gracie looked at a stunned Chubby and asked, "Seen enough, or do I have to put you in the tank with my Uncle KK?" Then, fixing her natural fearless stare, our gal Gracie said, "I have explicit top-secret information regarding all of this, and I know of you as O'Gooha Bhah Tootoe, a fine and honorable man. Let's go find Lucinda and Quinella." Chubby could only nod in agreement.

The Soup and Burger Emporium was nearly at full capacity, and, as you might expect, the lunch crowd was eerily quiet — lots of whispers, some finger pointing and a fair amount of noggin scratching. Merle was asked to manage and run the EMP for the next several weeks and did a good job of quashing all the stories and rumors about what may or may not have happened on that day.

Chubby was certain that the Bailarín twins had moved on and were no longer in the Monterey – Carmel Valley area. After a day or so, it was decided that Gracie, Kouba and Chub would head north towards Livermore, as had been suggested by "Him." They arrived late in the afternoon in San Ramon and checked in to the Bustado family's Bread, Bed and Breakfast. It was located close to Livermore's barrio section of town, which was convenient, as it was close to Lab #23.

After dinner, Chubby called a meeting in order to cobble together a plan to find and rescue Quinnie. Gracie reminded him, "We're also here to rescue Lucinda."

Our Zulu prince seemed somewhat confused by this revelation, but Kouba Kenta Bailey assured him, "Not to worry — it'll all be explained later."

Chubby said, "First we need to locate 'Packy the Pickle' and the other man who was occasionally seen with the Twins."

Right then they didn't have a lot to go on. So even in a high-tech comedy, mystery and love story like this one, our players were finding themselves as the future heroes who needed a lucky break. ("Whew," says Maynard, "it's about time.")

At about 10 p.m., Chubby and the gang drove down to the local Dairy Queen to get everyone a milkshake. Kouba Kenta had a hot fudge sundae instead. As they were leaving, who do you think pulled into the parking lot? "Packy the Pickle" — imagine that. The look on ol' Pack's face when he saw Chubby was worthy of a stand-in actor's honorary Oscar statue. He tried to back out but was blocked immediately by a finger-wagging Kouba. Our Chubster casually sauntered over to Packy's car and said, "Now son, you can get out of this piece-of-crap car you have driven up here by yourself, or I can pull you through the window or just simply rip the door off in one piece and drag you out. What's it gonna be?"

"I am getting out," said a shaken Packy.

"Good," said Chub. "Now we're all going over to our place at Bustado's and have a nice long talk. My pal Kouba will drive your junker so you won't have to walk back down here to the Dairy Queen when we're done. That's assuming you'll still be able to drive or walk."

Another car had just pulled in behind Packy and gone unnoticed except for a quick glance from Gracie. Turned out it was the clean-cut man who had been seen at the Pine Inn over in Carmel with the Twins. Apparently, he had an appointment with Packy.

Grace asked, "What about this guy?"

Chubby grinned his "gotcha" gold-tooth grin and said to her, "Go over and 'invite' him to the 'let's get to know each other' event at our 'cheese, wine and cracker' evening. Tell him we'll all have a good time there at the interrogation party. Where? Well, over at Bustado's — where else? Tell him he can ride over with Uncle KK."

Kouba Kenta Bailey wondered if they should also get some ice cream for the special guests. Probably not, eh?

Once everybody had made it to the Bustado family's Barrio, Bread, Bed and Breakfast Club, the process of information purging began. Packy was terrified, as was the other dude. Guess what, folks? A quick look at Mister Nice Guy's fancy haircut on his driver's licence revealed a name. The man was known as Dexter Lee Offenduzzem. Yep, same Dexter who was on Quinella's flight on the private jet to Los Angeles.

Boy, did he have some explaining to do, or what? Chubby communicated to the two men that it was now "Let's all tell the truth" time. He let it be known that, should they be caught in a lie, no matter how small or insignificant, there would be very serious consequences. The punishment would at first escalate in a linear fashion, before increasing in an exponentially and absolutely probably definitely for sure, no doubt about it, very painful way. He wanted to be perfectly clear about that.

Chubby demonstrated by snapping a thick hickory walking cane in half, pulling it slowly against his knee with both hands. *KREEK... KREEK... KREEK...... KER-RACK!!!* The Chubster looked at the two terrified, horror-struck men and said, "Any questions?" He reminded them that the sound they had just heard was very similar to a leg bone being cracked in half.

In a fearful, trembling voice, Dexter agreed to co-operate and answer any questions that he had information on. He said it was true that he worked for Casa Bailarín los Bandidos de la Sombra as a spy and had jumped ship from the Hasta Luego Cuanto La Gusta cartel. He knew that the latter group had a contract out on him for his life. He also realized that they were going to lose against the more powerful Shadow Dancers, as would all the rest of the rival controling organizations. Dexter said that he knew of the cosmic energy and powers that had been formed by an entity known as "Him" and was aware of those that followed "His" lead.

Packy hesitated for a moment, then looked at Chubby and said, "If I may ask a question, Sir — you are the only one that I have no information on. I am aware of Gracie Aylene and her mentor, Kouba Kenta Bailey, as well as Quinella and the amazing physical human blend known as Quinella Louise Fitzpatrick and Lucinda May Obermeyer McNichols, but I don't know who you are."

"Well," Chubby said, with a calculated, chin-scratching pause, "my name is Bond... James Bond." The silent hesitation being obvious, the ensuing laughter from everyone caused the nearby rolling hills to shift and bounce, as well as shaking every lampshade and all the kiddies' swing sets in the Hollister Valley. Why, it nearly straightened Kouba's seriously wavy white hair. Meanwhile, Gracie was busting her gut. (Sean Connery was desperately looking for Daniel Craig's phone number. Maynard just rolled his eyes.)

It didn't take long for things to get serious again as Chubby zeroed in on Packy and said, "Okay, let's have it, all of it, or you will become known within the Native circles of lore as Mister Packy the Pickle with Many Bones Broken Twice." Pack lowered his eyes, slumped over and said, "This is what I know, and it's all I know. Quinella is in the Bailarín Mansion over in San Ramon, which is about 25 minutes from here. You can't get to her, and even if you did, she has been drugged and has had a shrapnel-shredder bomb vest strapped to her body. The Twins had the explosive rigged so that it can be detonated via the Shadow Dancers' space satellite by cellphone activation. There would be nothing left of her."

Chubby decided that he would soon turn Packy and Dexter over to the CIA Special Services people, where no one would know their whereabouts. However, it was clear that the two men still had more information than they were willing to divulge right then. Looking over at Kouba, he asked, "Have you ordered a new battery for the cattle prod?" (Maynard thought that more information was forthcoming and probably right around the corner. ...Ya think?)

Chapter Nine

A New French Maid Dusts the Mansion

Meanwhile, at the Casa Bailarín Mansion, Quinella was overcoming the drug impairment and the surging influences affecting her. She knew how to purge and neutralize the negative reactions in her system through deep breathing and meditation. As she was coming out, she realized that she had to start acting as if she was still zonked. Being a fifth-degree black belt, she was totally aware that kicking the dickens out of her sleazy handlers would be a no-brainer and would only take a few seconds. The obvious barrier was, of course, the styled "fashionably correct" shrapnel-shredder bomb vest that was strapped onto her award-winning "Best of the Better Beach Babe Beautiful Bodies."

Well, would you believe that the jacket had an embroidery on its front? Yep, the Twins had a sick sense of humor, alright. You would recognize the logo right away as soon as you spotted the galloping pony in a stadium on a playing field of grass, chasing after this little white wooden ball. The rider appeared to be holding up something that looked like a croquet mallet, or perhaps it was a golf club, over his head. Quinella knew that she would have to be very careful, indeed. (Maynard says, "Ralph didn't think this was funny at all.")

* * *

After the interrogation of Dexter and Packy, Gracie got busy mapping out the Casa Bailarín Mansion, looking at blueprints acquired via the Internet from the Contra Costa County Courthouse in San Ramon. Its database covered all structures in the area. They all knew that something had to happen, or Quinnie-and-Lucinda were likely going to be cold, crumpled-up, shredded-up, bloody-burnt toast in a large mixing bowl.

Kouba discovered a service entrance at the rear of the building. It was likely that Quinnie was being held in a room upstairs not too far from this entry point. Grace came up with a brilliant plan — dangerous for sure if it failed, but easy and swift if it worked. This just might do it: Gracie would dress up as one of the housekeepers, complete with pink pleated silk blouse, white apron, really short miniskirt, black stockings and high-heeled pointy-toe shoes. A silly white lace headpiece would of course complete the chambermaid's fashion statement known as the "cleaning with feather duster" look. To validate the ruse, Gracie would also be carrying a mop, some towels and a bucket.

All of this garb was available over at the Sassy French Maid Shop on Garner Street, and they made home deliveries. Somebody would be there in about 15 minutes, as Bustado's was just across town. Imagine that.

By using the special powers that were hers alone, Gracie just strolled into the Bailarín Mansion as though she had been there for years. She located the two evil guards, who did not know they were holding both Lucinda and Quinella captive. How could they? She herself was still struggling to understand the bizarre concept of one body hosting the two-person package of Quinnie and Lucinda.

Gracie put all of that aside for a moment; then suddenly, in a blinding move, she snatched up the imbeciles by their ankles and stuck the jerks holding our "gals" hostage right into a life pause. All it took was for her to blink three times, point her two index fingers and one black Mary Jane shoe at them, and *ka-zap* and *ka-boink*, the guards were neatly frozen in time. It was so easy that she didn't even have to wiggle an ear.

It was time for Kouba Kenta to follow in and be a lookout while staying in touch with Chubby, who was standing guard next to the Raptor. Everyone had to keep in mind that one slip-up and it was all over.

Gracie was able to disarm the bomb vest by soaking it in Heinz ketchup, horseradish and mashed-up lima beans; the ketchup's acids compromised the wiring, thus neutralizing its explosive capability. We're still researching the effects, if any, of the horseradish and the beans. (Maynard says, "Ya can't make this stuff up.")

Okay, readers — not one of you has asked or pondered, "Just where did she get that much ketchup, horseradish and lima beans"? Perhaps this unusual and clearly surprising combination of ingredients came as part of a special shredder bomb vest removal kit that you could purchase separately. We understand that all of this was available at the BOMBS R US shop, owned by Danny Detonator (known as "Trigger-happy Dan" by his friends), over on Clacker Drive in San Ramon.

Well, after Gracie had successfully removed the vest from Quinella's torso, she got Lucinda/Quinnie out of the mansion and they rushed over to the Raptor, where Chubby was ready to hightail it out of there.

The most difficult part of this rescue was that Gracie had decided to undo and reverse the transformation and was now bringing Lucinda out and squeezing Quinella back into Lucinda's original body. It was a suggestion from "Him."

Once in the vehicle, the Chubster heard a *ka-pop!* — similar to the snapping sound of a can of beer being opened. Chub wasn't aware of it yet, but the person sitting behind him in the back seat was now no longer Quinella but had fully transformed back into Lucinda, whom he had never met. (Maynard thought it would have helped if Lucinda had stopped snoring so loudly. Well, it was irritating.)

Once again, Chub was blasting the Raptor towards Interstate 5 South. As things settled down a bit, he realized that there was an unfamiliar voice occasionally coming from the rear seat of the road beast. The Chubster adjusted his rear-view mirror and was shocked to see Lucinda, realizing that he did not recognize this person. And just where was his future lovey-bug, known as Quinella? Had somebody grabbed the wrong person? He pulled the Raptor off to the side of the freeway and said, "What in the fiddly-diddly doo-dah is going on here, and where is my gal?" Kouba Kenta looked up at the giant Zulu to explain, when Gracie said, "I'll handle this." It took a while, but faith and understanding were beginning to take hold.

Everybody had a gummy bear, which turned angst and fear into a "musical ear"-blasting adventure as the Raptor zipped down the freeway. They were singing along and loving the sounds of Fleetwood Mac, Eric Clapton, Bob Dillon, Elton John and Pink Floyd. Maynard and the rest of Gracie's Wacky Bunch were looking forward to the next selections on the playlist, especially the live concert recordings.

Don't worry, folks — Quinella will be back with us via some spiffy new wizardry. "He," who is "Him," has been holding back on us. Stay tuned. (Maynard says, "Nice going there, Mister Wannabe Author; let's see you get out of this one.")

* * *

Well, back at the Bailarín Mansion, all hell was breaking loose, as the most evil Twin, Chaco, couldn't revive the life-paused imbecilic guards, so he had them dunked into a vat of boiling all-polyester liquid. After a good hot soaking, they were fished out, blow-dried off, then mounted sitting on the mansion's upper-corner platforms to serve out eternity as well-dressed human gargoyles. They were so frightening that smarter pigeons and crows wouldn't dare fly near them. Those that did plummeted to the earth with massive coronary failure.

Since picking up dead birds was an unpleasant task, Beto Bailarín had baskets installed to catch the stupid ones, then set them on fire. Once a week, the caretakers at the mansion had torches going, which annoyed their law-abiding neighbors.

* * *

It was decided that Gracie, Lucinda May and Kouba Kenta Bailey would take up temporary residence in Quinella's cottage in Venice until a way to bring Quinnie back out, but without harming Lucinda, was decided on. A meeting was set up with "Him" down at the EMP so that Chubby could be involved in the plan.

While waiting for the bunch to show up, Chubby took a walk around the bar and lounge. He also toured the secret underground facility; he found it to be tidy, and at first all seemed okay. Merle was always off on Saturdays, so his absence was normal. However, there was soon no doubt in Chub's mind that something terrible had happened. He could feel it, because he was trained to sense the vibrations of this kind of an unbalanced environment.

The gang showed up, and both Gracie and Kouba Kenta realized something wasn't quite right, as well, but they couldn't quite place their focus in a way that coincided with Chub's reasons for feeling that something was very wrong.

Lucinda, who was in the Emporium for the first time, was standing at the bar, looking directly into the aquarium. Suddenly she asked, "Who's the cutie sitting on the Harley?"

Without knowing exactly what she was staring at, Chubby casually said that it was the skeleton of Garth McTavish.

"Well," said Lucinda, "guess what, folks — this here dude ain't no group of bones stuffed in a full-leather biker's outfit. It's a fresh gang-banger with freckles, big ears and curly red hair. Definitely no bones here."

For sure, it was a very fresh dead guy who was sitting on the bike. This realization created sheer drama and near-panic for all — it was a stunning reality to witness, to say the least. Perched in an all-out racing position and straddling the bike was Merle; he was wearing Garth's leathers, including his engineer side-buckle stomper boots and the classic motorcycle cap. Garth McTavish's skeleton was nowhere in sight. Describing the onlookers as "very quiet" at this moment would be a gross understatement. Closer inspection on Gracie's part revealed that a business card was attached to the front of the biker jacket. It read: "The Shadow Dancers."

A beeping sound was coming from the underground room. The wood-encased mirror with the swirling lavender clouds had just signaled in. A meeting with "Him" was about to take place. They all scrambled downstairs to await the arrival of "the Entity."

"He," who is known as "Him," appeared in the mirror, popped open his eyes and in a soft voice explained that he knew of the events that had taken place in the bar. "He," who is "Him," also instructed them not to worry and that a grand plan was in place to deal a major blow to the Casa Bailarín los Bandidos de la Sombra; it would in fact destroy them. The people in the room would be given instructions on how and when they would act together to bring The Shadow Dancers down.

"He," who is "Him," then continued, "I also have good news regarding Quinella Louise Fitzpatrick and Merle. She will be extracted from Lucinda's body, then refitted and fully integrated onto Merle's bones. His flesh, which is being preserved by the salt water, will be reworked onto Garth's skeleton (size matters), which has been hidden deep in the false cavern. Merle will then be electro-sparked twice, and — through the magic of genome reassignment — he will be returned to normal with new DNA and a fresh haircut. He will have a natural transition to a wonderful, healthy life. Quinella will be even more beautiful and powerful. She will now have her very own bio-vessel."

Chubby was thrilled as he stood in front of the wood-encased mirror. In a whisper, he thanked "Him" and said, "I, O'Gooha Bhah Tootoe, am your humble servant." The Entity in the mirror smiled, winked and responded, "We have much work to do," then vanished.

Suddenly a noise came from upstairs. Inside the fish tank, the sharks were racing each other, fiercely banging into anything in their way and wildly disturbing everything. It was pure chaos; fish were darting in and out, trying not to get run over or bitten by angry sea turtles. The octopus had managed to overcome her shyness. The manta ray showed up with a checkered flag, and the electric eel carried a placard saying "Garth must be returned, or else!!!"

"He," who is "Him," spoke to everyone in the fish tank in mako shark lingo and manta ray slang. "He" explained that a refurbished Garth McTavish skeleton would be repositioned onto the Harley-Davidson on the following Monday. Action in the tank calmed down considerably.

Chapter Ten

Vapor Domes of Death

Meanwhile, The Shadow Dancers of Casa Bailarín were planning the absolute takeover of the so-called civilized world, and soon. Their goal was to reduce the planet's population in order to achieve total power and global control in a more efficient manner. The way it was scripted was cruel, vicious and deadly.

First to be eliminated would be those incarcerated in the men's and women's prisons, municipal jails and mental institutions. Second would be the disabled and those with dementia. Next, the infirm and the senior citizens in rest homes and hospitals. In addition, all peoples in underdeveloped countries who were living in poverty would be wiped out. With only a few exceptions, all persons over 75 would be ordered to turn themselves in for cake, tea and sleeping pills — lots of pills. Finally, all non-essential animals such as pets would be butchered and used as a vital food source for the necessary continuation and maintenance of such enterprises as the dairy, beef and poultry industries.

None of this would be possible using the current military might or even with the use of nuclear weapons. Quite by chance, The Shadow Dancers had developed a secret new method of population reduction. This poisonous and invisible vapor had been discovered by accident while their lab, oddly enough, was seeking a cure for the dreaded chimpanzee black lung disease. The odorless vapor could be designed to encompass large areas of land using micro-management of measurable dimensions and encapsulating huge populations in one application.

The Dancers were able to develop specific targets through special screening, utilizing age-determining vibrations that were unknown to science. Those targeted would be turned into ash, grains of sand, and dust. The vapor would then just simply dissipate and go unnoticed as it was being air-washed back into the atmosphere. All of this was developed at the lab owned by Casa Bailarín los Bandidos de la Sombra.

In a less technical sense and for the layperson, here is how the lab found out about the discovery of the "Vapor of Death." First, there was the recognition of the elements forming the actual components that made the vapor into a usable contemporary weapon of mass you-know-what.

It had been known for years that "Plinkets," when separated from a jibbering of atomic capsules previously spun from the cake-like "Creedaschraam," would of course stretch and coagulate. They would then mollify themselves into thick "Duckets" of something very close to commercial mayonnaise. The fatal chemical combo, when heated, was subjected to a treatment known as "decarboxylation."

The transformed gel-like goo was then transferred via special automatic creeper-containers and loaded into firing pipes. Next it was all forwarded to a series of military tanks, battleships, aircraft and, in some cases, missiles to be launched at specific predetermined targets. When a "vapor bomb" was released in a coordinated, computer-controlled moment, the super-thin liquid cover surrounding it like a see-through veil, lifted and spread through the landscape, quietly encapsulating the target area. The vapor's outer surface looked like a giant, transparent, nearly invisible, soft plastic dome. (Maynard says, "Well, that's really laying a major literary load of certified crapola on the folks.")

Several small islands in the South Pacific were targeted for trial and evaluation. All of them had modest populations and were not under government scrutiny or subjected to the prying eyes of the news media. The testing was instant, successful and without a single burp or flaw.

Next, an ambitious and dangerous test was planned and designed to try and envelop a specific piece of real estate. The goal was to knock out India's largest prison, in Kolkata (formerly known as Calcutta). It was a very high-tech experiment requiring precise timing and measurements, which was difficult because of the name change. The new maps didn't match the old ones. Hmmm!!... (Potato, Patatoe, Oh Calcutta, Oh Kolkata.) Mentally, it puts you on the shackled edge of a purple clevis whistling softly through the sweet succotash of outer space... (Spatatoe, Spatatah?) (Maynard says, "Yep, he's losing it.")

The prison in India warehoused approximately 104,000 inmates, hundreds of guards and dozens of normal workers. In addition, all sorts of civilians would be visiting there every day. When the Death Vapor was released, it would go *crackle*, *gonk* and *poof,* instantly changing any life form inside the dome. The electronically programmed attack would trigger flashing bright lights and swirling vibrations of power, as if it had control of the sun. All at once, human and animal life would be reduced to ash, grains of sand, and dust.

On a Sunday at midnight, a violent, vicious act of terror did exactly that. *KAPOOT.* The buildings and their contents were left intact and unscathed.

There was a mention on the Kolkata nightly news about a disturbance at the prison, but not enough details were available yet to report much of a story. There was always chaos at the prison, anyway, so no big deal.

The media never bothered to follow up and discuss what had actually happened. The World Cup soccer games in New Delhi were way more important to the television producers and viewers and therefore got all the attention. About two weeks later, some official came forward with this phoney-baloney story. (Maynard says, "Look out, folks — government cover-up.")

Supposedly, the prison was going to be refurbished and the prisoners had been transported to other facilities. The official government account was that the records had all been lost due to a giant windstorm that had blown the papers here, there and everywhere. Everything had gotten seriously messed up. Locals were freaking out, dogs were barking at nothing and everything. Nobody knew just where anybody was.

All the shoulder shrugging caused massive neck injuries, resulting in ugly riots due to appointment booking and overloading with all the chiropractors, general practitioners and local snake charmers. The young and creative entrepreneur types quickly picked up the slack. They were getting rich by opening up hundreds of franchise businesses offering back- and neck-rubbing treatments while they lounged around in swanky parlors with super-hot babes, at times enjoying a toke or two of ganja through glass pipes.

Friends and frantic relatives of the vaporized inmates, guards and other employees were put on hold; as time went on, most of them simply gave up. ...Score one big hit for The Shadow Dancers.

* * *

Meanwhile, Lucinda, who had returned from California to the Rushtuk farm to meet up with Graham, was now getting reacquainted with her original body. The more she looked in the mirror, the more she liked it. However, she was a bit nervous about how Graham might see her. She was still very much in love with the handsome Senator from Idaho. She decided that she would just have to take her chances, as Graham had not seen her for several months.

Then Lucinda suddenly thought about her daughter. *How will Gracie think and feel when she sees me, now that I don't look like Quinella?* She realized that she didn't really need to worry about Gracie, as her daughter was already way ahead of everybody.

* * *

Before his wife's return to Rushtuk, Graham had arranged a meeting by phone with his golfing buddy, Judge Aaron K. Ledbetter, to see if he could get Lucinda a pardon and a criminal records expungement, as she had exhibited no symptoms that were connected to her past in almost a year. You might well imagine that, from his perspective, Dr. Hal Hankerbee wanted no more of Lucinda May in his life, for sure. He had signed off with the judge, giving her a "thumbs-up." As far as he was concerned, she had a clean bill of health and posed no threat to the public at large or to banks of any kind. He also gave her full credit for straightening out the poor quality of home delivery pizza. On a private note, Dr. Hal was still busy trying to come up with a cure for chronic adult bedwetting... Upon hearing the news, Gracie winked at Lucinda. *Meow-meow.*

* * *

The first thing Lucinda wanted to do was get together with Graham and plan a second honeymoon. She had missed him greatly. He was all for it and would be on holiday leave from the Senate in three days.

They both decided to go back to where they had eloped to after falling madly in love. So it was off to Tahiti, then the Hawaiian Islands, enjoying the sandy beaches and the sun. They liked Kauai the best, but all the islands were great. Two weeks of surf, sun, great food and lots of smoochy-smoochy. She darn near wore poor ol' Graham out.

Our Senator's face was about to fall off from smiling so much. He was like a lovesick badger who had just vaped a large Kona Gold nugget all by himself. He was also understandably confused, especially with all the rumors of body switching and stuffing between Quinella and Lucinda, and tales of both of them being rescued from those awful men who had threatened their lives. Graham was very interested in all of this, especially because he had never actually met Quinella. ...Hmmm.

Lucinda was still amazed by all the adventures she had experienced as Quinella. She wanted to know more about Graham's work in the Capitol, and did he know anything about these characters known as The Shadow Dancers? Well, he tried to answer Lucinda May as best as he could, but he really just wanted to relax with her. Smoochy, smoochy.

Graham sensed that his wife had changed somehow. She seemed stronger, as if there was another power source inside her. His senses had picked up on it; in fact, in their intimate moments, he was amazed at the difference in Lucinda's energy, and how much more playful she was. The shy, conservative woman he had married years before had noticeably changed. She looked, seemed and felt as he remembered; however, she was more creative, full of passion and wanted to try things that were new to both of them. It did not register intellectually with Graham what, if anything, had changed, but who in the heck was he to question all of this wonderful new excitement? Perhaps it was about time to just shut up and play the hottest new board game for lovers, called "OK, Dummy — It's Your Turn."

Well, there was obviously a lot to think about. Thankfully, however, Lucinda didn't snore anymore. (Maynard was relieved, as was Graham.) Keep in mind that this had nothing to do with her other reality in life, namely the personality changes. You might remember that her condition was clinically known as Multiple Personality Disorder. The medical name of this psychosis was changed in 1994 to Dissociative Identity Disorder, or DID. (Maynard says, "You probably didn't ask for it, but you're gonna learn a lot of psychobabble crap here, anyhow.")

On their way back to Los Angeles from Kauai, Graham received a message from his secretary to return to Washington immediately. He had hoped to visit with Gracie and Kouba Kenta in Venice for a few days first, and now that trip would have to happen at a different time. He was frustrated, as he also wanted to check out the Emporium and finally meet Chubby, as well as Quinella Louise Fitzpatrick. However, the truth was that Quinnie had vanished and there was no one to make soup and burgers at the EMP and serve customers. So Chubber had quickly convinced Lucinda to fill in for Quinella while she was in Venice. She could hang out at the beach cottage with Gracie and Kouba Kenta Bailey.

* * *

Before all of this was over, The Shadow Dancers were going to get a big taste of how powerful Lucinda May Obermeyer McNichols really was. Also, don't forget that she had inherited *Billions*, with a "B." This enormous wealth would become her personal war chest in the effort to defeat the evil Twins — Beto and Chaco Bailarín.

Graham had been selected to be on a new top-secret committee set up by the CIA, Interpol and MI6 to investigate the strange disappearance of large numbers of people in very different parts of the planet. The Shadow Dancers had been busy after the success of their Kolkata/Calcutta prison attack. The inhabitants who had vanished from the lower Pacific Islands, various mental institutions and senior citizen rest homes all over the globe had likewise succumbed to the "Vapor Domes of Death," proving that the plan would work. The

Dancers were on a roll, and something needed to happen right away, or it was going to be over soon.

It became clear to Gracie that there might be a chance to stop the evil momentum of Beto and Chaco. This, of course, would be a mission executed under the direction of "He," who is "Him." The tragic and brutal agenda set in motion by the evil Bailarín twins to control the world must be crushed, along with any of the remaining members of Casa Bailarín los Bandidos de la Sombra. They could not be allowed to continue.

A plan was hatched. "He," who is "Him," said that Gracie would have to return to San Ramon and continue with her duties, disguised as a maid and housekeeper. She was instructed to take Lucinda's long-handled makeup mirror with her so that communication with "He," who is "Him," through the swirling lavender clouds would be possible. Chubby would stay in Los Angeles for now. Grace and Kouba would drive Quinnie's Alfa Romeo Veloce up to San Ramon.

Gracie returned in a new "French Maid" costume to the mansion, where she informed the other employees that she had been transferred in from another Bailarín estate in Costa Rica. She was to assist in the management and restoration of this old mansion. They were told that except for the cook, the gardener, the groundskeeper and a security guard, all other workers would be put on holiday leave with full pay and benefits until further notice.

Gracie's first chore as the new manager was to hire a cook, a gardener and a groundskeeper. Her silly, straight "interviews" with Kouba Kenta Bailey for the jobs went well, as he had amazing credentials, so she hired him on the spot. He did want more benefits, but Gracie told him he would have to work there for six weeks with no demerits to qualify. As a goodwill gesture, she said he could continue wearing his chicken leg bone through the upper lip. They both howled with belly-cramping laughter. "He," who is "Him," was very pleased; "He" even smiled.

Chapter Eleven

Graham Gets Blindsided

Graham's flight back to Washington, DC, was painfully long and boring, even though he was allowed to travel first-class. A stunning and super-attractive flight attendant named Clara O'Donald caught his eye. She was paying more attention to him than would be expected. It was apparent that what she wanted and intended to do was to set up a casual in-flight relationship. She would make it appear as if it were an innocent effort to engage in a conversation that could easily happen. She was curious about his duties as a United States Senator. He just shrugged it off and thought to himself, *She just wants to flirt.* He was handsome and therefore used to it.

Graham was hungry, and he was ready to pig out. First-class passengers were always treated to a "fine dining" experience featuring the "rolled-up white linen napkin presentation," including quite heavy genuine silver cutlery. All served on plates made of real china — from China (where else?).

On tonight's flight, the gourmet selection consisted of fresh Maine lobster served with brushed-on, cannabis-infused garlic butter including a high percentage of CBD. In addition, from Nebraska, was a 12-ounce choice-cut perfectly marbled corn-fed filet mignon. The beef was chef-prepared and enhanced with stuffed peppercorns, then seared on both sides, leaving a hot-pink center. This mouthwatering "just off the ranch" delicacy was served with organic asparagus spears. They were covered with jalapeno-flavored hollandaise sauce and sautéed white mushrooms. All this was accompanied by a delicious tossed Greek salad.

Graham had a large glass of red wine, as he thought it might help him sleep. It came from the highly acclaimed Placido Picasso Winery. The 100-plus years-old vineyards were located just outside Madrid, Spain.

Well, nature called and he promptly got up to go to the lavatory, sometimes referred to as "the closet."

This was after slamming down most of the Picasso vino. He was about to whiz a "pee-pee" directly into the pants of his brand new hand-tailored $800 silk and wool Armani suit, when he realized that the Placido Picasso had problematically paralyzed and pre-empted his precarious predicament. Well, when he got to the bathroom door, he discovered that someone had accidentally locked it. It was an inside job, for sure. Graham was standing there, up on his toes, and was doing the back-and-forth, two-foot, ankle-busting, side-to-side, big-toe–twisting Texas bug-hustle shuffle, a popular dance at German beer gardens. He was trying his best not to dribble, spray or worse. An attendant hunted for a master key. Just in time, Graham got lucky: mission accomplished — whew! Some of the passengers applauded, others just smiled with respect. The rest thought the whole thing was an act and a disgusting put-on. They felt it was beneath the dignity of a United States Senator. (Maynard thought it was way too funny.)

Graham worked his way down the aisle, returned to his seat and found that Clara was now sitting in the seat next to his. She was smiling, teasing and wearing a "C'mon, big boy" smile. She held up a chilled bottle of French "Vinyé Vinyá." Graham knew that it was very rare and expensive. She explained that it was hers and she wanted to share it with him. Oh, by the way, the Captain had already dimmed the lights in the cabin down to a real low and silky-soft blue shade, creating a peaceful calm. The flight, already at 38,000 feet, was quiet and billiard-table–smooth. Most of the passengers were already snoozin' and cruisin'. They were still four hours out from DC. That's when Clara said she was on a return flight home and not on duty. She was just helping out, as the other first-class attendant wasn't feeling so hot.

Turns out, Clara and Graham got along really well, laughing and telling stories about themselves to each other. They continued to drink the wine, becoming very comfortable and somewhat schnockered. Well, let's tell it like it was — Graham simply got hammered. Clara especially loved his tales about when he lived in San Francisco near Haight-Ashbury. They roared with gut-busting laughter at the adventures he had experienced during his long relationship with his paranoid pet parakeet named Augie and the very large calico pussycat he called Spike. She also tried to imagine him as a long-haired hippie riding a Vespa.

Graham did notice that Clara wasn't too specific about her past. You know, the typical stuff — like suffering through piano lessons as a kid, being a cheerleader in high school, getting dumped by a boyfriend, going on to prep school in Philadelphia, then landing a job with the airlines, and, sadly, having wealthy parents who couldn't give a diddly-hoot about her. Clarence Wayne Darrow, her wealthy-lawyer older brother, got all the kudos. He was killer-handsome and played football and hockey and ran track. A star in all three sports. What did you expect?

Clara became quiet and Graham saw a couple of rainbow-colored tears tumble down off her cheek. He felt like a jerk for not seeing that one coming. His apology was heartfelt and genuine. She managed a smile and asked him to hand her a tissue from her jacket, which was between them. As he pulled a Kleenex out of her jacket pocket, a black business card flipped its way towards the floor of the aircraft. He reached down and caught it before it disappeared under her seat. As he was handing it to her, he noticed the name on the front. It read, "The Shadow Dancers."

"Is this yours?" he inquired.

"No," she said, "one of the passengers handed it to me as everyone was boarding. It was so busy I didn't pay much attention. It belongs to one of the twins sitting six rows behind us."

Huh? What? and *Eh?* Graham blinked twice and turned around to look, but there wasn't anybody six rows back and there were no "twins" anywhere in sight.

If this was a movie, you surely would be hearing the orchestra pounding the heavy notes and dramatic musical chords right now in a downward, rocket-powered motion, causing an ear-blasting crescendo. (Maynard was aware that all the sounds you would hear would naturally be quite far to the left side of Middle C. They would be very strong on the base notes — at least they were on his piano. *Dum-Dum, Da-Da, Dum-Dum, Da-Da, Clacka-Dacka-Whacka-Poon-Poon, Jahka-Roon-Roon.* A difficult singalong melody for all.)

Well, we are pretty sure it was the Thai stick. Or possibly the mushrooms. It was Dr. Francis O'Leary's "Pleasant Morning Sonata with a soft stroke and a deep toke for a lot of decent folk who like a good joke before they croak from silver moonlight smoke, in E Flat Minor." Now that's a tune for ya, Jasper. Former Governor of Texas Ann Richards had it right: "Poor ol' George, he cain't *hep* it." Remember now, "We cain't geh-eht no-oh sat-tish-fac-schun." It has been rumored that Governor Richards co-wrote this song with Mick. Ahem!!

Graham was polishing off the Vinyé Vinyá, when he suddenly noticed that this last glass of wine had a gritty texture to it. The smell was somewhat sour, and it had a very different taste from the other six or seven glasses he had consumed. There were little silver particles and a shadowy film of grainy residue sticking to the inside of the glass. He also noticed that Clara's glass didn't look like his at all.

A foggy sensation started to cloud the Senator's thinking, and he felt dizzy. His hands and feet were tingling and beginning to feel numb. His tongue was thick, making it difficult to speak. Hallucinations were filling up the spaces in his brain faster than he could process them. Graham was no stranger to drugs, but this one collected his entire being and was stretching all of his deeply rooted brain sockets.

He tried to focus on Clara, who was fixing a pillow for his head. She didn't look the same to him at all. She appeared ghoulish, with rotten, widely spaced, tobacco-stained teeth. She just watched with no emotion, no conversation, then waved the two men now suddenly seated six rows behind to stand beside her. Looking over her shoulder and staring at a very whacked-out United States Senator were the Twins, Beto and Chaco Bailarín. Graham slipped into darkness, and he would be that way for several hours.

The plane had long since landed and all the passengers and crew had departed. Graham was still out like a toasted zombie. Clara moved up into the officers' space with Beto and Chaco. Then she radioed the tower to get clearance for departure with a secret numbered FAA code. They all moved into the cabin to begin the long taxi crawl for takeoff. Clara sat in the First Captain's chair, with Beto in the other seat as the second in command and co-pilot. Chaco was to watch Graham and stay awake. He wondered what it would be like to skin out a United States Senator. The evil Twin broke out in a sweat just thinking about it.

The Boeing 787 Dreamliner roared down the runway, lifting off with lights blinking and looking very normal. Clara was a master at flying these jumbo jets. She had received her training as a Navy fighter pilot in San Diego and had flown dozens of missions over Southeast Asia during the 90s. They were climbing through some thin clouds with wheels now up and locked in place. The wings were trimmed and the engines throttled back. A smooth voice came into the cockpit over the PA system, speaking with a Middle Eastern accent, and said, "Have a nice flight, Shadow Dancers. We will see you in San Ramon and Los Angeles."

The massive Boeing 787 super-jet ripped back across the country, the engines being pushed to their maximum safe limits. This particular aircraft is capable of flying up to 200 miles per hour faster than the the speed at which the FAA allows regular commercial flights to operate. The descent into Los Angeles was routine and smooth. The big jet rolled over to a large, privately owned hangar used for maintenance on giant aircraft. The building was mysteriously dark. After a few moments, the engines were shut down and the plane was towed inside, followed closely by a brand new all black Cadillac stretch limo.

Several men dressed in white jumpsuits scurried around the exterior of the 787's belly as its huge lower bay doors slowly opened. (Visually, it was all eerily close to the James Bond 007 movies starring Sean Connery.) Being lowered to the floor by a Komatsu forklift were several wooden pallets holding securely strapped heavy metal containers locked in sequence in a two-by-two arrangement per pallet. Each very large aluminium barrel had a skull-and-crossbones insignia stamped on its side, signifying its poisonous contents. The barrels looked like jumbo beer kegs. The forklift struggled, as they were nearly twice as big as the ones that show up at frat houses across the country and obviously very heavy. It would take a full semester for that much beer to disappear.

Well, hold on there, folks. We understand that the University of Colorado accepted the challenge. (Maynard was seen washing his old college mug.)

That's, of course, assuming they were full of beer. They were not; what was in them was an assortment of basic chemical crystals, a brown powder of some sort and a tinted and very thin blueish liquid. They were the building blocks for making a gooey paste for the deadly Vapor Domes of Death.

The first-class passenger exit door swung open and the Bailarín twins emerged and hurried down the steps two at a time. It was actually quite funny to watch. It looked as if they were bobbing up and down doing the bunny-hop. *Bomp-a-bomp-a-dee-bomp, dee-doo-bomp, bomp-ah-dee-dee-dee-dee, do-dah-bomp... hop-hop-hop.* (Maynard says, "Best I can remember — you try it. Thanks to Ray Anthony and his 1953 big band sound.")

Following the Twins was Clara; she preferred one step at a time, as she had a carry-on bag that was quite bulky, in addition to Graham's briefcase with time-sensitive and top-secret material inside. Three very large Middle Eastern men exited the limo, carrying what looked like a heavy canvas sling with handles and a large zipper up the middle. Two of them went up the loading stairs into the jet and gathered up a limp, still unconscious Graham Reginald McNichols. He was unceremoniously stuffed headfirst into the body bag, then dragged over to the Caddy and tossed into the limo's massive trunk. Our Senator did not move a muscle; he could be kept like that for hours, still wrapped up in the sling and with no way to escape.

Clara climbed into the front seat and sat next to the driver, whose name was Farley Arkle. (All his friends and family would tease him and call him Farkel Arkel.) Beto and Chaco shook hands with the third Middle Eastern man. The three of them climbed into the limo and onto the rear "couch" next to the bar. The engine started and the evil-looking, tube-shaped black vehicle stretched itself even longer (or it seemed to) and moved into a lane headed towards the 405 freeway on-ramp, going north.

* * *

Graham was slowly waking up into a cold and pitch-black environment inside the large, uncomfortable trunk. It took a while to shake the bugs from his very confused thoughts. After extricating most of his body from the canvas sling, he noticed that all of his limbs were still attached and could function. He just couldn't see very much. He felt the motion of the limo and could barely hear the voices of Beto and Chaco.

Finally, Graham was able to wiggle himself free and away from the sling and started feeling his way around the spacious trunk. Well, guess what? Thanks to the engineering genius of General Motors, a very tiny safety light was mandatory for rescue reasons in case someone were to be trapped inside by accident — especially children, and occasionally pets. Right next to the light was a black lever with white lettering. The word "OPEN" was easy to read. Fortunately, he had enough presence of mind not to open the trunk lid while zooming up the San Diego freeway at 75 miles per hour.

The Senator would have to put an escape plan together quickly, as the limo would be exiting at the Westwood off-ramp and heading in towards

Beverly Hills. Graham put his head up against the rear firewall that separated the trunk from the back seat. He could barely hear the Twins talking, but he made out from their conversation that the limo would be pulling into the underground parking garage at the Beverly Wilshire Hotel. What the kidnappers didn't know was that the down-ramp was partially closed due to a construction project. They had to wait and be flagged in. The sheer length of the limo caused a further delay.

Beto and Chaco were in a hurry, as they wanted to catch a flight to San Jose, rent a car, then drive over to San Ramon and check out the strange and troubling rumors they had been hearing about what was apparently taking place at the Casa Bailarín Mansion.

The Twins decided to go on and leave Clara in charge of Graham and Farley the limo driver. Finally, the limousine was allowed into the underground garage, where it was parked in a hidden section near the elevators.

Farley said he needed a bathroom break and wanted to know if Clara would be okay with staying in the limo until he returned. Well, if there was going to be a chance for Graham to escape, this would be it. He waited two minutes, then flipped the lever.

The trunk lid popped open and rose upward in a slow and quiet way. Our Senator felt like a caged, cooped-up bird that had just been set free, and he was seeking revenge. After climbing out from the trunk, he headed towards the door behind which Clara was sitting. He wanted to break her neck but needed her for information. However, somehow he just didn't think she fit the picture of being a part of Casa Bailarín los Bandidos de la Sombra. But he had to be sure. It would later turn out that his hunch was accurate.

With Graham now fully recovered from the effects of the drug, it seemed to him that Clara had returned to looking the way she had always looked. He was grateful for this but wasn't sure exactly why. Due to all the construction noise, she was unaware that someone was poised and ready to yank open the door and break most of her bones. He wondered if she'd like to know what it would be like to spend some time in the limo's trunk. Why not — could it be all that bad? *He* had survived it. That seemed like a great idea; he would then wait for Mr. Farkel Arkel to return and give him the biggest surprise of his life.

Graham hustled Clara in an armlock to the rear of the limo and said, "You have a choice here. You can either climb in on your own, or should I put you in this canvas bag? After spending time in this trunk, you could find yourself to be in a lot of pain, with many bruises and broken bones. I would then zip you shut and you would be turned into a nice little 'tidy-tight' person who was formerly a lovely, intelligent, world-class gal and is now just a sad memory. You would be tucked right inside your very own sling."

A silent and terrified Clara O'Donald struggled to hide her fear as she stepped over the limo's bumper and into the trunk.

Graham continued, "Please do not harm the bag, because it will make a great souvenir. Later, I would love to hear your story, just before you say you're sorry, but I'm pretty sure your spanky-spunky self is going to be thrown into prison for life. Drugging and kidnapping a United States Senator is a rather serious issue, don't ya think?"

Well, Graham closed the trunk lid gently after removing the tiny light bulb that had set him free. Prior to Clara's entry into her new digs, he had also pulled out a classic 90-degree-angle, charcoal-colored tire iron from under the floor mat, where it had been firmly latched above the spare tire. Graham now gave the top surface of the trunk a rolling knuckle rap and said to her, "Not to worry, your eyes will adjust to the darkness, and when they do, well… it will be dark. Oh, just so you know, I wish you good luck, and thanks for shopping the wonders of my really nice newly acquired limo. I'll keep you informed — knock if you need anything."

Our totally energized Senator couldn't wait for Mr. Farley Arkel to come back and be required to give his comments on the design features of this very high-quality tire iron. Graham had decided that after each whack to Arkel's body he would ask for his evaluation, critique and scientific analysis. None of this emotional begging and whining crap. No sirree. No way, José. We just want the facts, Farley — just the facts. Graham wondered, for example: when one applies a sharp blow with the tire iron, would it be more painful to certain parts of the upper body, or would a chopping smash to the bridge of the nose possibly be more effective in getting the receiver's attention? Well, he thought, let's consider, for argument's sake, a nifty whack to the knees, or perhaps the shins, and — oh, yeah — how about the crotch? I'll bet that one smarts quite a bit. Oh really? Ya think? ("You betchum, Red Ryder." Maynard agreed, as he tried not to wince.)

Farley returned and was instantly shocked to discover that Clara was missing in action, as they say. The Senator slipped out from the shadows behind the elevators and gave Mr. Farkel Arkel the scare of his life. Graham shoved the tire iron crossways onto his throat and informed Farkel, "There are going to be some questions. Some could be very painful if not answered carefully and truthfully. Be advised that I have a small jar in my briefcase which will hold both of your precious 'loverboys.' Please don't make me slice them off. If I have to do that, it'll be both messy and time-consuming. You won't like it a bit."

By now Farley's eye sockets had stretched to the limit and were noticeably larger than normal. His deep blue peepers began shifting back and forth like the ball on an old IBM typewriter. He looked down at his shoes and said, "I am at your service, and thank you for rescuing me."

WHAT? EXCUSE ME?

Farley continued, "Chaco would have eventually killed me and my family. They're being held in a basement cell with steel bars across the front. No beds, no chairs, no nothing. The guards have been giving them scraps of food that I wouldn't give to a dog. My wife and kids have a five-gallon bucket for a toilet and wash basin. They've been locked up for weeks at the Bailarín Mansion."

Well, Graham didn't quite know what to do. He elected to put Farley in the back seat of the limo next to the bar and told him to open two beers. Our Senator had just come up with a plan. He had decided to let Clara out of the trunk and that they would all drive up to San Ramon. "Make that three beers, Farkel. Open the fridge and see if there are any chips and salsa — this is going to be a long night."

Graham opened the trunk and retrieved a very shaken Clara. "OK, cutie — I don't have much time, so would you please get in the front seat next to me and start telling your side of the story as we head to San Ramon. Tell it to me straight, or you'll make the trip up north back in the trunk."

Clara said she had nothing to hide and was sorry for what she had done. Chaco had threatened her with a death so horrific that it made Graham cringe. The evil Bailarín twin would usually hang his victims by their wrists or their ankles from a rafter in the basement of the mansion, then skin them alive with a chafing knife. He loved showing photos of his "work"; sometimes he would also play videos of what one could expect. He had once bragged that he could skin a body out in twenty minutes. (Maynard wasn't sure what the record was for a complete skin-out.)

Graham made a phone call to his office in DC to give "Duffy," his secretary, an update on his situation and also to ask why he was needed back in such a rush. He was stunned when she said that she hadn't called him and that he wasn't required to be back for any reason at all. Something was really funny here, and there had to be an answer to all of this. And of course there just might be.

Satisfied that Farley and Clara were being honest with him now, Graham felt more at ease and was reasonably sure that both could be trusted.

A sketchy bond, even a cautious friendship, between the three of them was taking place. (Maynard says, "Life can sometimes breed strange bedbugs, as well as bedfellows.") Acknowledging those thoughts, Clara reached into her coat pocket, pulled out a jumbo-size Maui-Wowie hashish-laced joint and said, "I'm sorry, but this is all I have. It will just have to get us to our destination — possibly somewhere, sometime, eventually, probably somehow, maybe anyhow." Then she murmured, with a possessed toker's grin, "Sharing enlightenment is always such a blessing." (Maynard says, "So twue, so twue," in agreement with his friend Madeline.)

Graham smiled, Farley Farkled his famous Farkle Arkle Sparkle and lit up the "fatty." The limo became filled with a sweet, pungent, floral aroma as Steely Dan opened up the limo's cozy environment — along with their eyes, ears, nose and throat — through the high-quality sound system with their blockbuster album *AJA* and other smash hits.

* * *

Back at the EMP, Chubby had things pretty much back to normal, but he was still disturbed about not being able to communicate with Quinella. Merle had been put on ice after being removed from the Harley-Davidson. A fake skeleton made of plastic had been dressed up in the biker leathers and stomper boots. As far as anyone knew, Garth McTavish had never looked better.

Chapter Twelve

The Shadow Dancers: A Final Waltz

Gracie, Lucinda May and Kouba Kenta Bailey were in complete charge of the Casa Bailarín los Bandidos de la Sombra mansion. They weren't prepared for a big surprise, but they were going to get one, anyway. The evil Twins, Beto and Chaco, had landed in San Jose after their one-hour flight from Los Angeles and were already in their rental car, anxious and working on a plan, driving as fast as possible straight over to San Ramon. All hell was about to bust wide open in a very few short hours.

Normally, someone from the mansion would be picking the Twins up. However, all the confusion and rumors about just who was in charge of the property had raised their awareness and suspicions to a very high level. They would use caution, stealth and sign language to ensure that the many entrances into the massive grounds and the labyrinth of secret passages had not been breached.

The mansion had long ago been designed for safety and security so that moving about through tunnels and other secret passages between walls would allow an assessment of what, who, when and where anyone was at any time. Listening tubes, peepholes and other recording devices were strategically placed throughout. This was in addition to several one-way–mirror viewing portals giving coverage of almost all of the mansion's interior. Audio and visual devices were also placed in and around on the grounds outside, further protecting the lush property.

It took several hours for the Twins to observe all that was happening and to devise a plan to capture and control the intruders. Beto Bailarín wanted them to face spending the rest of their lives locked up in the basement compartments, which were nothing more than modern versions of a medieval dungeon.

Chaco Bailarín had other thoughts, because he had just spotted Kouba Kenta Bailey. His mind was going *boing-boing* bonkers as he realized that he had an opportunity to skin out a pure white albino who was actually half black, with pink eyes and a massive top-heavy Rasta hairstyle and at least four very long dreadlocks. This would be his crowning glory as an artist, in a macabre and bizarre setting — a trophy that he would gloat over time and time again. Chaco could hardly contain himself. It would take hours to do it right, as he wanted to make Kouba Kenta Bailey's skin into a pull-on bodysuit. It would be a slipcover that he could put on and wear as a costume, or simply sit around in and watch TV. What we've discovered here is one notorious wacko-designated sick dude, folks.

Chaco was about the same size. After the removal of the "skin suit" from Kouba's body, he would first wash it down with alcohol, then he would soak it for three hours in a vat of heated lanolin. This procedure was to keep it from rotting or becoming stiff and brittle. He also had discovered that gentle rubbing and stroking with Arm & Hammer baking soda would keep the hide fresh, pliable and supple. He was surprised and pleased that this process would allow the retention of Kouba's creamy albino skin color.

The overall application worked. It also kept the houseflies and worms down to a minimum and likewise sealed the suit against smelling bad, either from aging or any other oversight regarding care. Chaco also planned to research getting eye contacts made in the traditional albino pink shade.

Using the digital texting feature on their cellphones, Beto and Chaco cross-checked the entire mansion several times in order to locate Gracie and Kouba. The pair, of course, had no idea that they were being stalked.

The Twins decided to create a diversion in order to separate Gracie from Kouba. Loud noises were heard out in the kitchen, followed by the sound of a cat meowing as if it had been hurt or somehow trapped under pots and pans. Gracie surmised that somehow a lot of kitchen stuff and assorted utensils had tumbled onto the floor. She told Uncle KK to wait in the parlor. "I'll go check out the noise, then meet you back over in the grand ballroom. Go ahead and light up the fireplace — it's chilly in here."

Kouba walked down the long, torchlit corridor and into the massive but elegant, art-filled grand ballroom. There were huge original 16th-century paintings mounted in large decorative wooden frames hanging along the full length of the walls. Across the expanse of the room were several classic statues of gladiators, Roman senators, Greek athletes and beautiful women; some were holding infants. These works of art had been purchased from famous collections over time. The Bailaríns had found that many of them came from Italy, Greece and Russia. Most of the statues were sculpted from marble or pure white alabaster. The taller ones were mounted on the floor, and others were perched on polished ancient teakwood tables. There were several fabulous ornate lamps, both short and tall.

The floors were randomly covered with the finest in Persian carpets, all handwoven from a blend of rich silk and wool, then reverse-knotted in the ancient and traditional methods of carpet making. The rugs in the mansion had been designed and made centuries before on crude but well-engineered looms. The production was meant primarily for sultans, mullahs and other royalty. Interestingly enough, there is a large collection of these irreplaceable works of art in the Vatican. The caliphs of Cairo eventually had to get theirs from local garage sales. (Maynard wants to know how we came up with that one.)

Sadly, these carpets represent a lost craft if you judge them by today's cheap technical standards. Today's "lookalike" versions appear as if they were pumped out of huge vending machines. The colors in the originals were stunning, and of course the rugs were priceless, as they were from a different era and therefore impossible to reproduce.

At the south end of the room was a one-of-a-kind grand piano made of burnished rosewood. Regrettably, the keys were made of real ivory. All of the rest of the furniture was masterfully arranged and faced the enormous fireplace. On both sides of the massive hearth were twenty-foot-tall custom-built bookcases including movable ladders that actually looked out of character and clearly were a late addition to the room. (Maynard says we will soon know the reason why.)

On the back wall of the room were two doors about 12 feet apart from each other. One was the door to a hallway connecting to six wine cellars; the other gave access to a large room where precut firewood was stacked and stored, along with other supplies.

Kouba Kenta walked across to the room where the firewood was. Carrying as many logs as he could, he moved over to the large opening in the fireplace and placed it neatly inside. He then stuffed bits of wood scraps and shreds of wadded-up newspaper in and around the logs. He always took pride in his ability to build a roaring and spectacular heat-generating fire that brought energy and warmth into any chilled room. He checked to see that the flue was open to get just the right amount of draft and draw. Control of the air was key to creating a lasting "snap, crackle and pop" evening.

When Kouba headed back across to get more logs for maintaining the fire, he noticed a whirring sound behind him coming from the bookcase on the left. A rush of cold air caused the fire to flicker and struggle to stay alive. Kouba turned and saw that the bookcase had rotated a half turn counter-clockwise. The stench from behind the opening was something that could have only come from some foul medieval dungeon.

Standing motionless in the opening of the bookcase was a well-groomed man in a dark suit with shiny, slicked-back hair and piercing, deep-set eyes. He was pointing a chrome-plated Colt 45 pistol right at Kouba's head. Uncle KK dropped his load of wood and raised both arms as high as he could. The dark figure moved into the room and motioned for Kouba to take a seat in one of the high-backed Queen Anne chairs. The sinister Twin cautiously moved closer and in a low voice said, "My name is Beto Bailarín — why are you in my house?"

Kouba's brain was processing a mile a minute, searching for a way to understand just what was happening. What could he do? What *should* he do? First, stay as calm as possible and not appear to be any kind of a threat to Beto. Kouba was normally pretty good in panic mode, but this was obviously just a tad over the top.

In a soft voice, Kouba explained that he was the new cook, gardener, household manager and errand person. He said that he had recently been hired and that there was a file in the office about who he was. He would be happy to show his credentials.

Beto growled and told him not to speak. At that moment his phone beeped. It was Chaco — he had spotted Gracie in the kitchen. He asked Beto, "What's happening in the ballroom, and what should I do after taking control of Gracie?"

Over in the kitchen, it took only a couple of minutes for Chaco to sneak up behind Gracie and wrap his arms around her. She had been so consumed by trying to locate what she thought was a cat that she presumed was in distress that she hadn't heard the Bailarín twin approach. Chaco spun her around, his face only inches from hers. The master of terror grinned once and meowed twice. He bound her wrists with his necktie, then wrapped the long end around her throat and said, "Let's go have a nice visit with your shiny white friend and my brother over in the ballroom. We would like to get to know you better. Oh, by the way, were you aware that you have very, very nice skin?"

Gracie knew that if she wanted to she could take Chaco down at any moment with her powers, but she was fearful that she didn't have all the information regarding Uncle KK's safety. She decided to go along and walked with Chaco peacefully back down to the ballroom to get a better assessment of the situation.

Beto looked at Gracie and said, "My my, what do we have here. A home invasion, perhaps a robbery, vandalism, snooping for secrets of some sort? It would be a good idea for you both to come clean right now, or I am going to let my brother Chaco sharpen his carving talents on both of you. Would you like to see some pictures of his work? There is nothing quite like it, I assure you."

Chaco kept observing Kouba Kenta, wondering just how and where to start. Would he hang him upright by the wrists, or by his ankles? He could make that decision later. There would be plenty of time for him to figure that out. He walked over to Kouba and said, "Take off your shirt. I want to get a reading on your skin's texture, tone and pliability."

The evaluation of skin thickness, along with age, had everything to do with achieving a professional result and obtaining the highest standards and desired qualities of a complicated strip-out. The evil Twin was happy that Kouba had very little body hair. He considered even moderate hairiness to be an unsuitable characteristic for skinning, creating a low-quality specimen that would therefore be beneath his talents. After all, the Shadow Dancer fancied himself to be a "top-shelf" artist, as well as a certified taxidermist.

Chaco was pleased with his new subject and said, "This is good — the thickness is naturally supple, moist and thus perfect. It looks like I can do this with a Victorinox six-inch skinning knife for the delicate areas." He also might use his latest butchering tool — called the Magnum Ulu Knife and used extensively in Alaska and Russia to skin out seals — along with the more traditional chafing blade, for removing the front and back larger "slabs." He knew that it also worked well on the buttocks, thighs and backs of the calves.

Still mesmerized by Kouba Kenta, Chaco continued, "I will have to assess this further, but it appears that you will do just fine. Don't worry, I won't destroy your Bob Marley Rasta look. I've always been fond of it, and his music. Perhaps we can listen to him as we work on getting you undone. My goal, of course, is to have you slip off as a one-piece bodysuit, very much like what the surfers wear while out in the ocean. I think I'll go with the 'solid front up to your neck, and the horizontal zipper across the back side of the shoulders' look. It then becomes a one-piece pull-on suit with a cleaner, more professional expression." The Twin could barely contain his excitement.

Chaco's evil gaze switched over to Gracie. In a sinister whisper, he said, "I can practise on little Miss cutie-curly sweetpie here. It's been a while since I've stripped out a teenager. I'll even let Mister Kouba Kenta Bailey watch. Heck of a deal, I'd say. Once I take some measurements, I'll order some new mannequins for stretching both your covers onto the forms. The ones I have now are stained and soiled and frankly stink a bit too much. I want everything to be fresh."

Beto said, "We're wasting far too much time here — let's lock them in the cell below the maids' chambers. We can decide what to do with them in the morning."

Chaco removed the long end of his tie from Gracie's neck and lashed her wrists to Kouba's. Then he marched the two of them down to the basement far below the ballroom.

At this point Beto motioned to Chaco and said, "Come on, we have to get ready for the Shadow Dancer team members to unleash the next Vapor Domes of Death, and soon."

The next mission was a very ambitious project indeed. The Casa Bailarín los Bandidos de la Sombra had decided on multiple geographic locations for their upcoming "Vaporization" of the unsuspecting masses. The island countries of Cuba and the Dominican Republic would be simultaneously targeted. Also included was the US territory of Puerto Rico. Based on information gathered in the past, the "useless ones" would be eliminated. The following day, the Dancers would also reach across to the Baja California Peninsula, using their member allies in Cabo San Lucas.

Once control of the smaller countries in the western hemisphere was complete, their plan was to tackle the more difficult areas, employing new strategic tactics to sequester the "unnecessary ones" and then eliminate them from the population base.

The Bandidos would start this second phase with Great Britain, then move on to Scandinavia. For now, they would not go after the countries south of Panama, which would of course include all of South America. The rest of Europe would also be put on hold.

Africa and the Middle East, as well as China, Indonesia and other Asian states, would be placed on the "catcha later" back burner. The Shadow Dancers were also gathering information on Russia and the satellite nations it controlled.

* * *

Kouba Kenta Bailey and Gracie sat quietly in their cell and waited patiently for the time being. They wanted to be sure that they were not being observed or recorded. They spoke to each other quietly and were careful to cover their mouths.

The Twins were focused and stayed busy, as they had just been informed via satellite that suspicious people were headed to the Casa Bailarín Mansion.

Yep, it was Chubby, Lucinda May and her hubby, Senator Graham Reginald McNichols, to the rescue. As a favor to the Senator, the Chubster had said that it would be okay to bring Graham's pets. I'm sure you all remember Augie the puffed-up paranoid parakeet and Spike the calico pussycat. Chubby suggested that they sit on the console between the front seats of the Raptor.

Once the gang were on the road, Spike wandered around inside the vehicle, getting hugs, catnip treats and belly scratches from everyone. Augie hopped up on the dash so that he could help drive and keep Chubby awake. He was also the designated entertainment director, with the responsibility for selecting the tunes for the trip. They listened to his selections on their way up to San Ramon. Augie was heavy into Carlos Santana, Fleetwood Mac and Neil Young. (Maynard said, "Ya gotta love those classics.")

Augie and Spike didn't know that anyone needed to be rescued. They just considered the excursion to be a family vacation. Chubby wanted to come clean and let the bird and the cat in on the facts. He was concerned that should they enter the mansion, they could fall into a trap with no possibility of a way out.

If only Gracie could contact everybody, including the animals, and warn them about what was going on, things might not be so dangerous. However, as you might imagine, Gracie's and Kouba's cellphones had been taken from them and getting out of the dungeon would have been noisy.

Through sophisticated satellite tracking devices, the Twins knew exactly when their uninvited guests would arrive at Casa Bailarín. They would be prepared to capture them easily. Chaco was so giddy that Beto told hm to go and take a Valium and settle down.

Chubby silenced the Raptor's engine as they were approaching the mansion and let the 4 x 4 super-beast coast over to a stop. Well hidden, he was now parked next to a grove of elm trees. The rolling and perfectly manicured lawns of the grounds lay between them and the castle-like front of the mansion. The building was mostly dark, with only a few lights on here and there.

Volumes of stifling stillness created waves of silence that were screaming in from every corner.

It was time to move forward and secure the target. Augie and Spike were instructed to remain in the Raptor until called upon and to raise the alarm if an unexpected threat should arise.

Completely unknown to everyone at the mansion was that at this very moment a CIA-owned Lockheed JetStar was streaking across the California desert sky, headed for San Ramon. It was flying under the radar and therefore undetectable by the Shadow Dancers' satellite.

Well, just who do you think would be at the controls of this slick pint-size super-jet? Yep, you guessed it — most of you, anyway. Anyone who didn't get it would have put this story down long ago. Okay, let us not lose the passion and energy that lies in front of us now. Clara O'Donald was clearly in control and was having a great time showing Farley Arkle all the gauges, switches and knobs and explaining what each one did. (A stunned Maynard asks, "Private jets have knobs?") Back in the JetStar's cabin, eating sandwiches, were Packy the Pickle, Dexter Lee Offenduzzum and Merle.

At the tiny San Ramon airport, officers Huh? and Uh-huh? had driven over from Monterey and were there to offer additional security if necessary. They were waiting to deliver the ready-to-go limo for

Farley and the gang. The jet was going to land in about five or six minutes — cutting it close, for sure, as Chubby and company would soon be entering the mansion near the maids' quarters. The Twins were watching their every move, pulling them into an easy trap where they could startle and attack our heroes. Gracie and Uncle KK had been moved by one of the guards from their cell through the dungeon and up into the gigantic ballroom. Farley's wife and kids would join them.

Gracie needed to be at her very best if she intended to turn this whole thing around and get control. Everything was quiet as a mouse; the Twins were present but out of sight for the moment. They would have the advantage of surprise. Beto was hidden behind the rotating bookcase, and Chaco was lying down inside the grand piano.

Chubby instructed everyone to be totally silent as they entered the large room. A quick glance from Gracie to our Zulu guy let him know that all was not well.

The bookcase rotated and Beto jumped out, firing two shots into the celling. Simultaneously, Chaco leapt from the piano and fired two shots as well. Beto shouted for all to sit on the floor now, or he would shoot the children.

Everyone obeyed. ("Alrighty then there now," as Jim Carrey might have said.)

"To what do we owe this unannounced visit?" asked Beto. "Please feel free to speak. We have all day. You will soon find out that coming here was a big mistake."

* * *

Meanwhile, Clara, Farley, Dexter, Merle and the rest of the gang were moving in at a fast pace. The Twins had no clue.

The rescue group gathered at the Raptor, where they were greeted by Augie and Spike. Gracie had been communicating with the pets telepathically, using her knowledge of bird-chirp speak and cat-meow talk. A plan was quickly hatched and everyone had an important role to play.

Augie hopped up on Spike's shoulders, and the courageous clan of misfits marched forth. No one knew about what Augie and Spike were going to do. They would show to all a feat so dramatic, so strong, that no one would believe it, even if they were to see it with their own eyes.

Now that they were almost at the front door, the clan was about to witness the most amazing unnatural event in natural history. Spike took a deep breath and curled his tail in a knot while Augie narrowed his eyes to slits, allowing intense super-focus. The pumped-up parakeet opened his beak for air and dug his talons deep into Spike's considerable coat of thick fur. Next, Augie started flapping his wings at an ever-accelerating pace. As the flapping became faster and faster, loads of dust and gravel launched into the air. A wind-turbo–like sound grew louder and louder. Calico Spike hunkered down into a take-off stance that would have garnered respect and high marks from any seasoned fighter pilot.

All this was possible because Augie and Spike had practised for weeks out in the barn up in the loft. They would fly around for hours, perfecting their aerobatics and other special maneuvers until the parakeet was exhausted.

"Now!!!!" screeched Augie. The bird and cat blasted through the massive wooden front doors right into the ballroom. They were flying at amazing speeds, swooping up and down, banking side to side, dive-bombing with amazing accuracy. Everyone was stunned, to say the least. The Bailarín twins could only stare. They were frozen and couldn't even fire off a single shot; the flying cat-and-bird duo owned the moment, saving not only the day but possibly the civilized world.

Quinnie shoved Beto and Chaco over to Chub after knocking their pistols to the floor. Farley had put his wife and kids under the grand piano. Dexter Lee Offenduzzum and Clara grabbed fireplace tools and started swinging them towards the Twins. They planned to raid the wine collection after the skirmish and drama was over. But of course. What else!! (Maynard says, "Count me in.")

Chubby saw his opportunity and grabbed the Twins, lifting them off the floor by the backs of their suit jackets. He slammed them together, then let them crumple down to their shoes, still well-dressed but with the strength of Jello. The rest of Clara's bunch had followed in and made sure that no one else was in the mansion.

Augie let Spike down gently before flying over to Graham and sitting on his shoulder. With bleary, bloodshot eyes, the bird asked, "Can we go home now?" They were both disappointed that they had forgotten to bring their signature flying capes and goggles. The Senator said not to worry, it would be corrected in the movie.

Gracie and Uncle KK decided to go to the kitchen and make sandwiches for everyone. Merle, on the other hand, along with Packy the Pickle, took charge of putting a stop to the Shadow Dancers' preplanned attacks. They got on the Internet and ordered the captains of Casa Bailarín los Bandidos de la Sombra to cancel the countdown and not fire up the Vapor Domes of Death. All members were told that a new plan was taking place and that they needed to get to San Ramon as quickly as possible for briefing. No exceptions.

With that, our Zulu king walked over to Quinella and said, "Babe, you are the greatest. Hows about going to dinner sometime?" Quinnie blushed and said, "Sure, how about that nice little hotel over in Carmel? I'm told they have a great appetizer bar and a lovely fountain."

Merle and Clara decided to hop on the JetStar and fly back to Los Angeles. They wanted to make sure that the aquarium at the EMP and its occupants were all okay. Gracie and Kouba returned to the ballroom, where Augie and Spike sat next to Gracie at the piano. She soothed the mood in the mansion by playing sweet melodies for several hours. Graham, Lucinda May and Dexter Lee Offenduzzum took turns stoking the fire.

Epilogue

Gracie Aylene McNichols walked over to the center of the ballroom and asked for everyone's attention. She smiled and said, "I'm so proud of the bravery shown by all. I really want to continue going after the 'bad guys' in our world. But first I want to finish my education at home, and especially get back to being captain of the volleyball team at the University of Idaho in Pocatello. I've also decided to offer the position of co-captain to Melissa Slipindonker — she deserves it."

Grace continued, "Augie and Spike need to have a normal life, and my parents, Lucinda and Graham, have their retirement years to start planning for. Kouba Kenta Bailey, who is my love, my mentor, my coach, needs to have a future of his own. Having said all of this, I must bid you all a farewell and a good life."

Gracie took a deep breath, blinked three times, wiggled her ears and pointed one final black Mary Jane shoe at the rotten, evil Bailarín twins. She raised her arms up high and waited for the sudden signal. Her body began to twitch, shimmer and glow. She was in cosmic concert with the lightning and the rolling thunder outside the mansion. Everyone was surrounded by an intense and pulsing white light. Then, there was quiet — just warm, mellow, swirling-lavender silence.

Poof, Gracie was gone. The rest of the group all agreed that she must be headed towards the Arizona desert to meet once again with the silver fox. You know — the one with the emerald green eyes. He had been waiting for her. After all, it was "He," who was "Him."

* * *

Well, folks, you could say that this adventure was over, and I would certainly agree. One small problem: Remember all those mental vibrations that Lucinda May Obermeyer used to experience? Do you recall the psychotic personality disorders that took place, turning her into someone else?...

Well, do ya?... There was Dottie Monet, the bank robber, and Nelda Zaffley, world-renowned concert pianist. They will be sorely and forever missed, but not forgotten.

Acknowledgments

I would like to thank the many personal friends who encouraged me and the professional people who worked tirelessly to bring this book to completion and out there for you to endure and enjoy. First and foremost, Anne Ryall, who did the copy editing, among other major duties. Next, Larry Shwedyk, who created the incredible artwork on the front cover. Then Tiffany Meyer, who was a genius at combining the various elements so that the illustration expresses the spirit of this endeavor. Colleen Campbell artfully created the landscape background for the cover. A big thank you to my family for their assistance, and to my delightfully rowdy friends — Darcey-Lynn and Bob MacArthur, Mike Gould, Wayne and Sandy Grams, Billy Cardoza, Dr. Terry Wilmot, Jim Lillard, Clint Causey and Bob Snape — who supported me and provided inspiration for the book. Maynard continues to bravely set the standard and supplies constant leadership (he is, of course, the itinerant man of knowledge).

About the Author

This is Richard Wyly's second book, following his equally humorous *The Saga of Stickitville*, both under the banner *Tales of Wonder*. Richard has enjoyed entertaining others ever since he was about two years old, when he began belting out classic American folk songs while taking center stage on the family coffee table. He grew up in Roswell, New Mexico, spending much of his childhood on the farms and ranches of relatives. His extensive background in the apparel industry dates back to when he began working for his parents in their children's clothing business at age 10. A former vintage car racer, motorcycle enthusiast and marathoner, he currently lives in Canmore, Alberta. Visit Richard's website, RichardWyly.com, and watch for future *Tales of Wonder* titles.

Fast Cars... Fast Women!

English

Dick Wyly

My Dog

My dog sats in the sun,
while he shines his paws.
He sats and hums
and waits for night to come.

By Dick Wyly

**An early literary effort
from little Dickie Wyly**

Lola T-160 at speed... Palm Springs

When racing through a high-speed corner to the point of losing adhesion, you will be suddenly forced to learn about the physical disconnect from gravity. It's known as "drifting." Assuming you don't crash, you can choose afterward to mentally convert this experience to the thought process of remembering. If you set your memory of your last lap in slow-motion mode, you can feel the vibrations and the sounds — and the euphoria, albeit frightening. It's a window into a new reality.

After returning to your racing pit, you might want to look down at the driver's seat, and — lo and behold — you will see a pinched and definite upward pucker in the leather, which is where the cheeks of your butt have grabbed onto for dear life. In racing circles, it's called a "cleach mark."

Sweetheart Run, Playa del Rey

All running is good. Long-distance running, in my experience, is better. It doesn't have to be fast, just long, at a comfortable pace. Anything beyond, say, an hour or so, gets you into the category of LSD — Long Slow Distance. In most cases, the body will respond to the task set by its owner; that's its job. Of course, this doesn't happen overnight. Some get there faster than others. Volumes have already been written on how it works, so I won't go into that right now.

I am always grateful for the hundreds of times over my forty years of running that I have personally experienced the so-called "runner's high." I was able to get my body to a fitness level where a special awareness was a dependable reality. The smile on my face was reward enough for me.

My marathon days are probably behind me now that I'm 80, but my commitment to fitness will always be with me, until I go *phissstt* or *phoose*. Whichever — it doesn't really matter.

Richard Wyly in his backyard

CPSIA information can be obtained
at www.ICGtesting.com
Printed in the USA
BVHW042343310820
587629BV00007B/13/J

9 780228 831716